World DANCE ACADEMY

TILLY'S TIME TO SHINE

Also available in the WEDA series:

Billie's Big Audition

TILLY'S TIME TO SHINE

Kimberly Wyatt

EGMONT

EGMONT
We bring stories to life

First published in Great Britain 2017
by Egmont UK Limited
The Yellow Building, 1 Nicholas Road, London W11 4AN

Text copyright © 2017 Beautiful Movements Ltd
Cover illustration copyright © 2017 Beautiful Movements Ltd

The moral rights of the author have been asserted

ISBN 978 1 4052 87180

67252/1

A CIP catalogue record for this title is available
from the British Library

Typeset by Avon DataSet Ltd, Bidford on Avon, Warwickshire
Printed and bound in Great Britain by the CPI Group

Stay safe online. Any website addresses listed in this book are correct
at the time of going to print. However, Egmont is not responsible for
content hosted by third parties. Please be aware that online content
can be subject to change and websites can contain content that is
unsuitable for children. We advise that all children are supervised
when using the internet.

For my nieces Alyson and Gracyn

CHAPTER ONE

It aws teh best of tmies, ti wsa the wosrt fo timse, ti was teh age of widsom, it aws the aeg of foloishness, it wsa the epohc of beleif, ti was teh epoch of incerdulity, it was eth saeson of lihgt, it was the season fo dakrness, it wsa the spirng of hope, ti was the witner of depsair.

Tilly stared at the words until her eyes burned and her head hurt, but the letters kept jumping about all over the page.

'What are you supposed to say?' Tilly pleaded with the letters. But it was no good, they still wouldn't fall into their correct order. 'I hate you, dyslexia!' Tilly threw the worksheet on to her bedroom floor.

It was so unfair. Nine out of ten people *didn't* have dyslexia. Why did she have to be the one who did? At her last school she'd been given extra support in class, but since she'd got to WEDA she'd been trying to make out that she didn't need it. She definitely didn't need the other students feeling sorry for her or, even worse, making fun of her. Now, as she looked at the paper on the floor, she wondered if she'd been right to hide it.

Before Tilly and her fellow students at WEDA had broken up for the Christmas holiday, their English teacher, Mrs Jarvis, had given them 'some fun reading for the holiday'. Apparently, the printout contained some of the best opening paragraphs of books ever written. But to Tilly, they might as well have been written in Chinese. She wished Billie was there to help her. Billie was the only person at WEDA she'd told about her dyslexia. Whenever they got set English assignments during term time, Billie would read them out loud for her. At least then she was able to understand what the jumbled-up letters meant.

As Tilly thought of her friend Billie, miles away in London, she felt a pang of sadness. If only Christmas was over already. Tilly frowned. You were supposed to feel homesick for your home, not your school. But for Tilly it was the other way round. In her first term boarding at WEDA she'd come to think of the dance academy as her home and her friends in her street crew, Il Bello, as her family.

Tilly got off her bed and walked over to the full-length mirror on her wardrobe door. She didn't feel like herself when she was here any more – not her true self, anyway. She gazed at her reflection, at her bland brown hair and her pale, make-up-free face. She hated looking so colourless and plain, and how vulnerable it made her feel. But her parents didn't like her dyeing her hair or wearing make-up and she didn't want to do anything to annoy them right now.

Her mum had been really disappointed with Tilly's first end-of-term report. Even though Tilly had got a glowing report in all of her dance classes, her mum was only interested in her academic grades. She was a lawyer and obsessed with how Tilly did in things like Maths and English. It had been hard enough getting her mum to agree to her going to WEDA – so if Tilly had to look like a boring loser to keep her mum happy over the Christmas holiday, it was a price worth paying. Tilly ran her finger over her cheek. Her skin was as lumpy as a mountain range. *G-reat*, she was about to have another break-out. Her spots always got worse when she was stressed, which only made her more stressed – leaving her in a vicious, spotty cycle. She glared at her reflection. *I hate you, spots! I hate you even more than I hate dyslexia!* She grabbed her concealer from her make-up bag, then remembered that her mum didn't even like her wearing that. She took the cap off the concealer and drew an angry face with it on the mirror instead. Then she added a lightning bolt and a thundercloud. Tilly stepped back and grinned. Channelling her feelings into artwork always made her feel better.

Twenty One Pilots came on the radio and, instinctively, Tilly struck a pose, tilting her head back and extending her arm. Voguing was her favourite way to dance. Like her artwork, it always made her feel better. There was something so therapeutic about the angles of the poses and the tension in her body creating such sharp lines. She took a step to the side, landing on her English assignment. The sound of the paper crunching beneath her foot made her smile again. She liked the power it gave her. She wanted to trample and stomp those stupid, jumbled-up words into the ground.

Tilly spun and twirled and vogued her way around her bedroom using the crumpled piece of paper as a skate on the carpet to help her glide. She caught sight of her reflection in the wardrobe mirror. She no longer looked sad and boring. Her eyes were sparkling and her cheeks glowed. One of Tilly's teachers at WEDA, Mr Marlo, called this feeling Doctor Dance. No matter how bad things might get, dance always made you feel better.

Tilly put her hands on her hips and stared back at her reflection.

'You've got this,' she told herself. 'You don't need anyone's help.'

She grabbed her fake fur coat and studded leather rucksack from her bed and headed for the door. Time for some Christmas shopping.

Tilly's family lived in a town south of London. Normally Tilly found it super boring, but today even she had to admit that it looked magical. The high street was strung with flashing, star-shaped Christmas lights, and the wide pavements were full of market stalls selling everything from French cheeses and wine to designer jewellery and handmade cards. Tilly picked out a couple of cards for her parents and her older brother, Bobby, then headed down one of the side-streets to her favourite charity shop. Tilly *loved* charity shops. Browsing through their racks and shelves was like treasure hunting – you had to sift through a load of junk, but Tilly had a knack for finding the gems. Her friend Andre loved this about her, because she was always finding weird and unique outfits for his fashion blog, Spotted. Tilly felt another twinge of sadness as she thought of Andre. He was even further away than Billie, spending Christmas in his hometown of New York.

The bell above the shop door jangled as Tilly made her way inside. The air had that slightly musty smell that all charity shops have, mingled with the spicy scent of a Christmas candle. She made her way to the women's clothes section and started rifling through the jumpers and blouses. Straight away, Tilly's mind filled with brightly coloured pictures, as she imagined snipping a sleeve off a shirt, or layering a vest top over a jumper, but none of the clothes passed the tingle test. The tingle test was something she and Andre always used for Spotted.

Unless an outfit was so exciting it made their skin tingle it wouldn't make the cut. But then she saw a hat, randomly perched on top of a pile of records. It was an old-style captain's hat, huge and black with a curved rim. Tilly picked it up and turned it over in her hands. There was so much blank space on the black felt – it was just begging to be customized! She pictured the hat covered with pink, black and gunmetal sparkles. She imagined gold chains hanging down from the rim around her face. Her skin began to tingle. She took the hat over to the counter to pay.

When Tilly got back home her parents were still out, picking Bobby up from uni, so she set to work at the dining-room table. In her first term at WEDA she'd collected loads of accessories customizing things for Andre's blog, and had bought a vintage trunk to store them all in. She opened the trunk and piled paint, glue, glitter and costume jewellery on to the table. Then she took out a pack of strawberry bubble-gum and popped a piece in her mouth. Her parents hated her chewing gum in the house, but it helped her to think. She placed the hat in the middle of the dining-room table and stared at it, waiting for inspiration to strike. This was how she always worked when she was customizing something, or creating a look. She didn't need to try out different things – she could see the finished look straight away. Andre called it her styling superpower. And sure enough, as Tilly stared at the hat, she saw an image start to appear on the front, like a Polaroid picture developing. The image was of a bright pink flamingo – it would go so well against the black of the hat! She imagined it glinting and shining in the light, and reached for her bag of Swarovski crystals and a tube of pink paint. Then she grabbed the hat and a pencil and started sketching the outline of a flamingo on the front. Tilly LOVED flamingos. Not only were they her favourite colour – pink – but they had long legs, like her.

When Tilly was younger, a bratty girl at her school called Angelica had constantly taunted her about her long legs, calling her 'lanky' and 'daddy-long-legs'. Tilly finally snapped and got her revenge by squirting ketchup into Angelica's school bag one lunchtime, which, of course, had got her into loads of trouble. But when she'd told her dad why she'd done it he'd said something she'd never forgotten. 'You're not a daddy-long-legs,' he'd told her, as he gave her a hug. 'You're my fearless flamingo.' Tilly loved her dad for saying this. Flamingos were way cooler than daddy-long-legs and they made her feel proud of her body instead of embarrassed.

Within a couple of minutes the outline of the flamingo was complete. Tilly blew a satisfied bubble with her gum and kept on blowing till it popped. The rest of Il Bello loved watching her draw and paint. They always made a big deal of her graffiti murals in the old stable they used as a studio. But to Tilly, art came easy – a bit like words came to them, she guessed. Oh well, at least there was something she could do that the others couldn't. She painted in the outline of the flamingo in pink and while she was waiting for it to dry, she took a photo of the hat and texted it to Andre. He texted back straight away.

OGM! That si so goign no SPOTETD! Xoxo

Tilly stared at the words until she finally figured them out – OMG! That is so going on Spotted! Xoxo

She sent back a smiley-faced emoji. Tilly was so grateful for the invention of emojis. If only she could do her school work in them!

Once the paint had dried, she began gluing the crystals around the outline of the flamingo. She pictured dancing in the hat on a stage somewhere, a spotlight casting reflected beams from the crystals all around her. She was so engrossed, she didn't even hear her family arriving back home until Bobby walked through the door.

'Sis! It's so good to see you!' he cried, dropping his bag to the floor and throwing his arm round her shoulders. Even though it had only been three months since Tilly last saw him, his hair was a lot longer and he looked older somehow. Uni life clearly suited him, but then Bobby was a brainiac just like their mum. 'What are you up to?' He nodded at the hat. 'I hope that isn't Dad's Christmas present – I'm not sure pink's his colour!'

Tilly burst out laughing. Their dad was an accountant who specialized in corporate taxation. Tilly wasn't exactly sure what that meant but she knew it sounded seriously *boring*. And her dad had a seriously boring wardrobe to match, spending his entire life in grey suits or brown cardigans. The thought of him wearing the flamingo hat was hilarious!

'What's so funny?' Tilly's mum came through the door smiling, but as soon as she saw the dining-room table, her face fell. 'Oh, Tilly, what a mess!'

'She's being creative,' Bobby said, instantly slipping into his usual role as the family peacekeeper. 'Look at the flamingo she's made. Isn't it cool?'

'It's ridiculous.' Her mum sighed. 'Who would ever wear such a thing?'

Tilly felt a red-hot rush of anger. *I would!* she wanted to yell. But she managed to stay silent.

'I have a ton of work to do, Tilly,' her mum continued. 'I need you to get this mess cleared away immediately.'

'It's not mess,' Tilly muttered. Then she had an idea. Maybe if her mum saw some of her finished creations she'd be more impressed. She picked up her phone and did a quick search for Andre's blog. 'Look. Here are some of the things I've made recently.' She showed her mum the phone. 'I put the braiding on those trousers and I added the pink fur trim to that coat.' She waited nervously for her mum to respond.

Her mum stared blankly at the screen. 'And when exactly did you do this?'

'When I was at WEDA – in my spare time.'

Her mum frowned so hard two sharp lines appeared in her forehead between her eyes. 'You're supposed to be *studying* in your spare time, not playing dress-up or arts and crafts. No wonder your grades were so low!' She handed the phone back to Tilly. 'I knew it was a mistake sending you there. I said to your father that –'

'It wasn't a mistake!' Tilly interrupted, her stomach churning. 'I love it there and I'm doing really well in my dancing.'

'I don't care about your dancing!' her mum snapped. 'Once you're out in the real world it'll be your academic exams that count.' She folded her arms and stared at Tilly, the way she always did when she was done talking.

'But you don't understand,' Tilly blurted. 'I find it so hard to concentrate! It's not my fault I have dyslexia!'

'But you told me your dyslexia wasn't much of a problem any more,' her mum replied. 'That was one of the reasons I agreed to let you go to WEDA.'

'It isn't. I – I was just using that as an excuse . . . for my grades.' Tilly's face flushed. Whatever she said now, she'd end up busted. She might as well avoid the dyslexia conversation.

'Right, so clearly you aren't trying as hard as you should be.' Her mum sighed. 'I mean it, Tilly – if

you don't get your academic grades up next term,
I'm taking you out of WEDA.'

CHAPTER TWO

Tilly walked into her dorm room at WEDA and gave the world's biggest ever sigh of relief. It was so good to finally be back – it had felt like the Christmas holiday would never end. But as she looked around her side of the room – at the bed crammed with cushions in every shade of pink and the brightly coloured mood-boards hanging on the wall – the relief she felt was tinged with fear. Her mum had reminded her yet again of her threat to remove her from WEDA when she'd dropped her back at the academy. 'I meant what I said, Tilly,' she'd repeated as they got out of the car. 'If you don't get your grades up this term, we're moving you to a normal school.'

Tilly sank down on to her bed. She couldn't go to a 'normal' school. She wasn't normal, and she didn't ever want to be. WEDA was the first place she'd ever felt free to be her own quirky and expressive self. She looked over to the other side of the room. There was a half-unpacked suitcase on the other bed, with clothes spilling out of it and on to the floor. Her roommate Naomi was obviously back, and there were no prizes for guessing where she'd be. Naomi's twin brother Jordan was also at WEDA, so she spent most of her time in his room. Normally, Tilly liked this as it gave her loads of space to be on her own. But after the holiday she'd just had, being on her own was the last thing she wanted.

It was weird – even though she'd been with her family the whole time, she'd still felt all alone. Bobby had spent most of the break on Skype to his girlfriend or playing Xbox games with his mates, and their parents might as well have been on another planet, wrapped up in their work or talking about the news. Tilly had spent the entire holiday feeling like a jigsaw piece in the wrong puzzle. She jumped to her feet and looked in the mirror on the back of the door.

'Time to be me again,' she said to her reflection, before grabbing a pack of hair dye from her bag.

One hour later, Tilly looked back at her reflection and smiled. Her sharply bobbed hair was now fiery-red, her eyes were lined with black kohl in a perfect cat-eye and her skin had been smoothed out with a layer of foundation. Like a warrior dressed for battle, she felt ready to face the world again. She applied some rose-tinted gloss to her lips and pouted. She was about to pull a pose when the door burst open and Andre marched in. He was wearing a bright green tracksuit, lilac high-tops and a baseball cap with *BORN BEAUTIFUL* written in diamante around the rim.

'Oh, thank God!' he exclaimed. 'If you weren't here I think I might have actually cried . . . and that would have totally ruined my look. Red eyes so do not go with green.' He came and stood behind Tilly and looked at her reflection in the mirror. 'Babes, your hair is fetch!'

'Thank you! It's so good to see you, Dre!' Tilly turned and hugged Andre tight. As always he smelled amazing – a mixture of coconut oil and cocoa butter.

'How good?' Andre pulled back and stared at her.

Tilly frowned. 'What?'

'How good is it? To see me? On a scale of one to ten?'

'About fifty million.'

Andre breathed a sigh of relief.

'Why?'

He shrugged and looked away. 'Oh I don't know. I thought maybe after some time away from here you might have gone off me.'

'What? Why?' Tilly stared at him in shock. It was totally out of character for super-confident Andre to show any sign of self-doubt.

Andre sat down on the edge of her bed. 'Tillz, can I ask you something?'

'Of course.'

'Do you like being my friend?'

'Are you being serious?' Tilly sat down next to him.

'Why did you say that?' Andre stared at her. 'Why didn't you just answer the question? Were you trying to avoid answering the question?'

'Dre, chill! Of course I like being your friend! I *love* being your friend. You have no idea how much I missed you over the break.'

'Really?'

'Yes! Now why are you being so weird?'

Andre took his cap off and sighed. 'Let's just say I didn't exactly have the happiest of holidays.'

Tilly gave a wry laugh. 'Join the club!'

'Really?' Andre looked at her hopefully. 'Did you have a lousy time too?'

'You could say that.'

'Oh good!'

'Andre!'

'Sorry. I didn't mean – I'm not glad that you had a lousy time. I'm just glad that I wasn't the only one.'

'But how could you have had a bad time? You were in New York!'

'Yes, and so was my so-called dad.'

'Oh.' Tilly wasn't sure what to say to this. Andre never talked about his dad, apart from saying things like his dad was dead to him and that he'd rather have a cardboard cut-out of Dr Dre for a father.

'Why did you have a bad time?' Andre asked.

'My mum was stressing over my end-of-term report.'

'What? But you aced your dance classes.'

'I know. But she doesn't care about that. She only cares about how I do in my academic subjects. Total nightmare.'

Andre sighed. 'Parents!' He put his cap on back to front and held his hand out to Tilly. 'Come on. I know something that'll cheer you up.'

Tilly followed Andre out of the ultra-modern dormitory block and past the old WEDA building. It looked so majestic, lit up in the dark.

'Where are we going?' she asked, and then it

dawned on her. 'Oh my God, is it ready? Are you taking me to the stable?'

'That'll be the official street dance Stable Studio,' Andre said with a grin. 'And yep, my mum said they completed the refurbishment over the holiday.'

As Tilly followed Andre through the cluster of trees at the back of the building she felt excitement bubbling inside her. Last term, the old abandoned stable at the bottom of WEDA's grounds had become the secret HQ for their street dance crew. But then Andre's mum, Miss Murphy, the world-famous ballerina and now Head of Dance and Wellness at WEDA had caught them rehearsing. They could have got into massive trouble, as street dance wasn't on the curriculum back then and they were banned from rehearsing privately when they had a show coming up. But thankfully Miss Murphy had been so impressed by their routine she'd allowed Il Bello to perform in the end-of-term showcase *and* street dance had been added to the curriculum at WEDA. The old stable had been renovated over the Christmas holiday to make sure it met studio health and safety regulations. Tilly couldn't wait to see what it looked like. As they approached the stable, Andre took a key from his pocket.

'My mum wants you to paint a sign for over the door.'

'Seriously?'

'Yeah, she loves your work.'

Tilly felt a burst of happiness, swiftly followed by a pang of sorrow. Why couldn't her mum be more like Miss Murphy and appreciate the things Tilly could do instead of picking holes in those she couldn't?

Andre opened the door and flicked a light switch.

'Oh wow!' Tilly gazed around the stable. The main wall was exactly as they'd left it, with Tilly's mural of Il Bello and the street-style bumblebees. But the wall opposite was now fully mirrored and the remaining two walls had been painted white.

'My mum asked if you'd do some more murals

there too,' Andre said, gesturing at the blank walls.

'Of course,' Tilly murmured. She looked up at the ceiling, which now twinkled with mini spotlights, casting a golden glow over the shiny pine floor.

'So, what do you say we dance out our holiday blues? Have a 'rent vent on the floor?' Andre said.

Tilly grinned. 'I say, YEAH!'

Andre went over to the brand new stereo system and put his iPod on.

As the Jack Garratt remix of 'Photograph' began to play he dimmed the lights and closed his eyes, his face serious again. Tilly joined him in the middle of the floor and waited for a couple of bars, letting the rhythm of the song work its way inside her body, then they both started freestyling through and around each other. It was as if their bodies were talking to each other, both anticipating and understanding what the other was saying. Expressing the same frustrations. Then, as the music built, they broke away from each other and started dancing to their own flow. Andre started moving robotically but gracefully, as if he were carrying a load of heavy rocks. Tilly vogued with a contemporary twist, her body flowing like a river. As the song came to an end they leaped into a hug.

'I feel so much better!' Andre exclaimed.

'Me too,' Tilly said and to her horror, she felt tears of relief burning in the corners of her eyes. She blinked hard and turned away. She hated crying, especially in front of other people. She was fiercer than that. She was a fearless flamingo, not a cry-baby.

'You OK, Tillz?' Andre asked.

'Yeah, I'm fine,' Tilly replied quickly.

'*Sei bellisima*, Tilly. Always remember that.'

'What does that mean?'

'It's "you're beautiful" in Italian,' Andre told her.

Tilly's face flushed. She felt so happy to be back where she belonged, with people who really got her.

'Speaking of which, we'd better get out of here and get some beauty sleep.' Andre went over to the stereo and retrieved his iPod. 'We've got a big day ahead of us tomorrow and I'm going to be trialling a new F Dot look.'

Tilly frowned. 'What does F Dot mean?'

'First Day of Term, of course. Wait till you see it, Tillz. I got a green Marc Jacobs skull and cross-bones bandana at a thrift store in Brooklyn that's to die for. And that's not even an exaggeration, I actually did almost die for it. I was so eager to get to it I pulled the whole shelf down on top of me.'

As Tilly burst out laughing she felt overwhelmed with relief. All of the tension that had built up inside of her over the holiday had been danced and laughed out of her body. She was back at WEDA and this term she was determined not to blow it. She was going to do whatever it took to get her grades up and keep her place there – and she was going to beat her dyslexia once and for all.

CHAPTER
THREE

The next morning Tilly woke bright and early. She hopped out of bed, being careful not to wake Naomi, who was still burrowed under her duvet, fast asleep, and unrolled her yoga mat on the floor. Tilly liked to stretch and breathe first thing in the morning, checking in with her body, figuring out which muscles needed attention and filling her lungs with new air. The rhythm of her breath, and connecting it to a stretch, was the best way to get rid of any sad cobwebs and start fresh. After dancing with Andre her left hamstring felt a little tight, so she soothed it with some gentle downward-dog stretches, sending her breath to the sore parts of her body and feeling the tension gently release. Then she showered and took her make-up bag down from the shelf. She decided to go for a bright green cat-eye this morning, to celebrate the first day of the new term – or F Dot as Andre called it! She wondered why Andre had been so stressed when he'd first come to see her. She hated thinking of him having a tough time over Christmas, it made her feel really angry. She always got like this when someone she loved was hurting – she was as fierce and protective as a lioness with her cub.

Naomi stretched an arm out of the duvet. 'What time is it?' she murmured sleepily.

'Almost time for breakfast,' Tilly replied happily. That was another thing she was glad to be back at WEDA for – the amazing food. The chefs in their canteen had a magical ability of making even the healthiest of foods taste delicious.

'Drat!' Naomi muttered and burrowed back beneath her duvet. Naomi loved saying 'drat'. She thought it made her sound distinguished.

'Come on, you know you want one of those

yummy coconut flour pancakes,' Tilly said. 'Just think of it, with some fresh, juicy blueberries on top. And a dollop of mascarpone – so creamy and delicious and –'

'All right, all right, I'm getting up!' Naomi flung back her duvet. Her dark hair was flattened on one side where she'd been sleeping. 'I hate these early morning starts,' she moaned as she shuffled off to their shared bathroom.

Tilly grinned. The only good thing about having a rubbish Christmas break was that it made her so happy to be back at WEDA she didn't even mind getting up early. 'I'll see you in the canteen!' she called after Naomi. She couldn't wait any longer, she wanted to see the rest of Il Bello.

The canteen was buzzing with chatter as the other boarders all clustered around tables, catching up on each other's holidays. Tilly spotted a tall, thin boy in a fedora hat standing at the juice bar.

'MJ!' she called as she ran over, fighting the urge to hug him. MJ was autistic and wasn't a great fan of being touched, or of displays of affection. Like Tilly, he expressed himself best through dance.

MJ turned and gave her a tight smile. 'Hey, Tilly. How are you?'

'Great, thanks. So happy to be back here.'

MJ nodded. 'Me too.'

'Are any of the rest of the crew here?' Tilly turned and scanned the canteen.

'Andre's still in our room trying to get his hair symmetrical – whatever that means – but Raf's over there.' MJ nodded to a table in the corner.

Tilly grinned as she saw Raf looking more tanned and handsome than ever . . . then frowned as she saw Cassandra sitting next to him, giggling and swishing her hair.

'What's he doing with the ice queen?' she asked.

MJ looked at her blankly. He didn't get metaphors.

'Cassandra. Why is he sitting with Cassandra?'

MJ shrugged. He hadn't got into any of the tension that had built up between Tilly, Billie and Cassandra last term. He tended to stay on the sidelines – until it came time to dance. 'Billie's just arrived,' he said nonchalantly, before turning back to the juice bar.

'What? Where?' Tilly looked around and spotted Billie by the doorway to the canteen. Her blond hair was tucked up inside a blue beanie and she was carrying a sports bag over her shoulder. As a non-boarder, Billie had to make a two-hour train journey to get to WEDA every day. She must have set off extra early this morning to make it in time for breakfast.

'Bill!' Tilly yelled, racing over to her.

Billie dropped her bag to the floor and ran to meet her. 'Tillz! It's so good to see you!' she exclaimed as the two girls hugged. 'How was your Christmas?'

'OK. How was yours?'

'It was great.' Billie's eyes sparkled and she grinned excitedly. 'My Uncle Charlie came to stay and my mum's new boyfriend Tony took us to see the fireworks on the Thames on New Year's Eve. It was so much fun!'

Tilly felt a bittersweet mixture of happiness for

her friend and regret that she didn't have such a fun Christmas break herself. Why did her mum have to be so serious the whole time? They'd spent New Year's Eve doing a family quiz which, as far as Tilly was concerned, was just one small step away from doing an exam.

'I'm so glad to be back, though,' Billie continued, linking her arm through Tilly's. 'I really missed you.'

'Me too,' Tilly replied. She took off her backpack and pulled out a present. 'Here, I made you something while I was home.'

Billie stared at her, puzzled. 'But I thought we exchanged gifts before we broke up?'

'We did.' Tilly grinned. 'This isn't a Christmas present.'

'What is it then?'

'It's a thank-you-for-being-the-best-friend-ever present.'

'Oh, Tillz!'

Tilly watched nervously as Billie opened the wrapping paper and pulled out a black T-shirt.

Tilly had printed the word *BILLERINA* in hot-pink graffiti lettering on the front.

Billie's mouth dropped open in surprise. 'That's what my Uncle Charlie calls me! How did you know?'

'I heard him call you it after the end-of-term showcase.'

Billie grabbed her in a hug. 'Tillz, this is one of the best gifts I've ever been given.'

'Really?'

Billie nodded. 'You're the most caring, thoughtful friend ever.'

Tilly gave an embarrassed grin. 'Yeah well, don't tell anyone. I have my reputation to protect, you know. Come on, let's get some pancakes.'

After breakfast, the students all filed through to the main hall for Mrs Jones's traditional start-of-term speech. Along with Mr Marlo and Miss Murphy, Mrs Jones was Tilly's main source of inspiration at WEDA. She'd been one of the founders of the academy and had taught Miss Murphy, who often credited Mrs Jones with her success. Tilly felt a flutter of excitement as she thought of how lucky she was to be there. Her mum might be dismissive of dance but Mrs Jones, Miss Murphy and all the other teachers at WEDA were proof of how successful dancers could be. Tilly needed to hold on to that thought and use it to keep her strong.

Andre, who hadn't shown up for breakfast, came rushing into the hall and plonked himself down in the seat next to Tilly. His F Dot look had clearly taken a lot of effort, but it had definitely been worth it. He was wearing a bright red vest top and black cargo pants and he'd shaved two perfectly symmetrical skulls on either side of his head, which went brilliantly with his green skull and cross-bones bandana.

'You look amazing,' Tilly whispered. 'With your green bandana and my green cat-eyes, we make the ultimate superhero duo.'

'I know,' Andre replied. 'I think this might just be our FFM.'

'What does that mean?' Billie asked from the other side of Tilly.

'Finest Fashion Moment, of course,' Andre said with a sigh.

Tilly laughed. If anyone else said such a thing they'd seem arrogant, but Andre was so funny he got away with it.

'Ooh, here we go,' Andre said, as Mrs Jones, Mr Marlo and Miss Murphy came in.

The students fell silent as the teachers walked to the front of the hall. Miss Murphy and Mr Marlo sat down and Mrs Jones went up on to the stage. She was wearing one of her trademark long dresses, in a deep plum colour, and her white hair had been cut into a graduated bob. It really suited her heart-shaped face. Tilly hoped she looked half as cool as Mrs Jones when she was that age.

'Good morning, everyone,' Mrs Jones said with a smile. 'And welcome back. I hope you all had wonderful Christmases . . . but now the party's over and the hard work begins.'

A few of the students gave mock groans but Tilly felt like cheering. She couldn't wait to get back in the studio.

'At the end of last term some of you were involved in a showcase at the Royal Albert Hall.'

Tilly and the rest of Il Bello looked at each other and grinned.

'I'm proud to say that you were an absolute credit to WEDA and gave it your all, but this term, we're going to be asking you to give even more than your all.' Mrs Jones looked around, her expression now deadly serious. 'I'm going to hand over to my colleagues Miss Murphy and Mr Marlo and they will explain.'

'What's up, WEDA?' Mr Marlo boomed. 'How you all doing?'

The students yelled back at him.

'I hope you all had a cool Christmas,' Miss Murphy said. As usual, she looked immaculate, in a long grey pencil skirt, crisp white blouse and sky-high heels.

Andre groaned. 'I keep telling her not to say cool,' he muttered. 'It's so uncool.'

Tilly laughed. As far as she was concerned, Andre had the coolest mum in the world – she'd give anything to have a mum as passionate about dance as Miss Murphy – but she guessed that, no matter who your parents were, you were embarrassed by them.

Mr Marlo dug his hands into his tracksuit pockets. 'As Mrs Jones just said, this term we're going to be asking even more of you than we did before.'

'We're going to be asking you to dig deeper than ever,' Miss Murphy said.

'And dance like the world's depending on you . . .' Mr Marlo paused for a moment, '. . . because in a way, it is.'

'Here at WEDA we need to become more energy efficient,' Miss Murphy said. 'And as part of that initiative, we need to install solar panels to the studio roofs.'

'But solar panels cost money . . .' Mr Marlo said.

'A lot of money . . .'

'So that's where you guys come in.'

Miss Murphy stepped closer to the edge of the stage. 'This term, we're going to be having an investor showcase to try to raise more funds for WEDA, so that we can pay for the refurbishments we badly need so that we can continue to run in line with our healthy and sustainable ethos.'

'And fund some more bursaries so that more dancers are able to enjoy the opportunities WEDA offers, whatever their background,' Mr Marlo added.

Tilly looked at Billie and grinned. Billie wouldn't have been able to come to WEDA if it weren't for the bursary system.

'So, what do you say?' Mr Marlo boomed. 'Do we have your commitment?'

'Are you willing to go that extra mile?' Miss Murphy asked, looking out at the students.

A few claps and whoops rippled around the hall.

'I can't hear you,' Mr Marlo said, cupping his ear.

This time loud cheers rang out.

'Bravo! That's more like it.' Mr Marlo smiled. 'Seriously, guys, this is your opportunity to give something back. Not just to WEDA but to the environment and to students less fortunate than you.'

'I personally can't think of a better motivation to dance,' Miss Murphy said.

'Me neither.' Mr Marlo nodded in agreement. 'And on that note . . . what do you say we have a welcome back West African drumming session? I've got some friends warming up the Djembe in the Murphy Studio as we speak.'

The students burst into applause.

'All right!' Mr Marlo yelled. 'Let's dance!'

As Tilly entered the Murphy Studio, every cell in her body tingled. Now she truly was back at home. As the students all found a place on the floor, a group of drummers in the corner of the studio started pounding out a rhythm on the Djembe. Tilly closed her eyes and let it reverberate through her body. She loved African dance. She loved that it was so raw, and the way it made you feel part of a team, a family. And she *was* part of a tribe – the WEDA tribe. She could feel the energy from the other students seeping into her as they began to dance. She allowed herself to sink deeper into the rhythm, letting herself go until there was no boundary left between her and the music. It was as if her body had become an extension of the drum, and she felt lit up with happiness. This was where she belonged – on a dance floor, expressing herself with her body. With every pound of the drum she felt an even stronger connection with her warrior within, and more determined than ever. This term she was going to dance as if the world depended on it, because it did. Her world depended on her staying at WEDA.

CHAPTER
FOUR

'Welcome back, everybody!' Mrs Jarvis called out from behind her desk as Tilly and the rest of her class filed into the classroom.

Tilly had been dreading returning to her English class, but the echo of the Djembe drums was still pounding away inside her, making her feel strong. She sat down next to Billie and took a deep breath. *You can do this, girl,* she told herself. *You can beat this stupid dyslexia.*

'I hope you all enjoyed the reading I set you over the holiday,' Mrs Jarvis said. 'Today we're going to look at what makes a great beginning to a story, so you'll need the handouts I gave you.'

Tilly's stomach churned. Her handout had been

so crumpled and torn after she'd danced on it, she'd ended up throwing it in the bin. Mrs Jarvis hadn't said that they'd need them again. She'd said it was just some 'fun reading'. She glanced around the room as everyone else got their sheets out. At the table across the aisle from her, Cassandra took her handout from her expensive leather bag. It was pristine in a plastic folder. Great.

'Do you need to share mine?' Billie whispered, placing the pages on the table in front of them.

Tilly nodded and gave her a grateful smile.

'OK, to start off I'm going to go around the class and ask you to tell us which of the openings you enjoyed the most.' Mrs Jarvis got up and stood in front of her desk.

Tilly felt her chest tighten. What was she going to say? She hadn't read any of them! As her classmates took it in turns to share their favourite extract, she wracked her brains for an excuse as to why she hadn't read any. She looked down at the handout on the table. The letters jumped around the page as if they were as nervous as she was.

'Which one was your favourite, Billie?' Mrs Jarvis said.

Tilly felt sick. It would be her next.

'A *Tale of Two Cities* by Charles Dickens,' Billie replied. 'I loved the way he kept talking in opposites. Like, right from the very beginning when he says, *It was the best of times, it was the worst of times* he grabs your attention. Straight away I wanted to know what he was talking about.'

'Excellent,' Mrs Jarvis said, smiling warmly at Billie.

Tilly couldn't help feeling a little jealous. Billie enjoyed English so much – she found it so easy – and Mrs Jarvis loved her for it.

'How about you, Tilly?' Mrs Jarvis said. 'Which was your favourite?'

'That one,' Tilly muttered.

'Which one?'

'The one that Billie just said.'

'*The Tale of Two Cities?*'

'Yes.' Tilly heard Cassandra sniggering across the aisle. *Don't get mad*, she told herself. *Even if that smug know-it-all deserves to be thrown head first in the bin. Stay calm.*

'And why was it your favourite?' Mrs Jarvis asked.

'Because I liked how he did that best and worst thing too.' Tilly squirmed. She sounded so dumb.

Mrs Jarvis looked at her for a moment. She wasn't smiling any more. 'And what else did you like about it?'

'What else?'

'Yes.'

Tilly froze. Why was Mrs Jarvis asking her that? She hadn't asked Billie for more things she'd liked. 'Erm . . .' She stared down at the page. The jumbled-up letters seemed to be taunting her now, forming themselves into a secret code she'd never be able to crack. 'I – er – liked the words he used.'

'Which words?' Mrs Jarvis asked.

Tilly's face began to burn.

'You did read the handout over Christmas, didn't you?' Mrs Jarvis stared at her.

'Y – yes – I –' Tilly stammered.

'Did you have trouble reading it because –'

'No!' Tilly practically yelled. She took a deep breath, trying to compose herself. The last thing she needed was Queen of Smug Cassandra thinking she couldn't read. She'd spent all of last term convincing Mrs Jarvis that she didn't need any extra support for that very reason. 'Of course not.'

'We were talking about how much we liked the word "epoch", weren't we, Tilly?' Billie said.

Tilly nodded, even though she didn't have a clue what epoch meant. She hadn't even heard the word before.

'And "incredulity",' Billie added, nudging Tilly's leg with her own, under the table.

'Yes, I love the word "incredulity",' Tilly said lamely.

Mrs Jarvis nodded but she was frowning. 'OK, thank you. How about you, Cassandra?'

'I found it so hard to choose!' Cassandra said in a

sickly sweet voice. 'Would it be OK to tell you about my *two* favourites?'

'Of course!' Mrs Jarvis's smile returned.

Tilly felt sick. She'd been so determined to do better in English this term. Billie gave her a sympathetic smile but, even though she'd tried to help, Tilly didn't want Billie's help and she didn't want her pity. She didn't want to talk about stupid words and stories. She just wanted to dance.

The rest of the day followed the same pattern. Tilly would go to a dance class and feel happy and confident, then she'd have an academic lesson and all her stress would come flooding back. When classes finally finished for the day, Tilly trudged through the grounds to the Street Dance HQ at the Stable Studio. She knew she should have been excited at the thought of dancing with Il Bello again but it was as if a black cloud had gathered above her, growing bigger with every lesson, and she just couldn't shake it off. As she reached the studio her phone buzzed. Her heart sank as she saw it was a text from her mum.

Hi, jsut wanetd to see how yuor first day
wnet. I hope you rembemered what I siad
and made a rael efofrt in your calsses. Mum

Tilly stuffed the phone back in her bag. Was this what it was going to be like from now on? Her mum breathing down her neck all the time? Haunting her by text message?

'Hey, what kept you?' Andre said, as she hurried into the studio. The others were all there already, warming up in the corner.

'Sorry, I got kept behind in Maths.' Tilly hurried over to join them and took off her coat.

'Are you OK?' Billie asked.

'I'm fine.' The words came out a little more sharply than Tilly had meant and Billie turned away, clearly hurt. Tilly didn't mean to be grumpy, but she didn't want Billie bringing up what had happened in English. Being with the crew was her escape – the one place she could truly be herself again.

Billie took her warm-up jacket off. She was wearing the T-shirt Tilly had made her underneath.

'Awesome top!' Andre exclaimed.

'Tillz made it for me,' Billie said. MJ and Raf gathered round her to take a look.

'Billerina.' Raf read the graffiti-style lettering in his strong Cuban accent and grinned. 'Cool name.'

'It's what my Uncle Charlie calls me,' Billie explained. 'Tilly overheard him and printed it on the T-shirt.'

'The way you designed the letters is sick,' Andre said, turning to Tilly. 'Seriously, Tillz, you're so talented.'

'She's the best,' Billie said with a smile.

As the others all nodded in agreement Tilly felt the stress from the day ease a little, and she let out a sigh. 'It's so good to be back with you guys.'

'Tell me about it,' Andre said, gesturing at them all to come closer. 'Group hug?'

They huddled together in a circle and grinned at each other.

'To Il Bello!' Andre said.

'Il Bello!' the others echoed.

'Here's to a new year of being fearless and authentic and our true selves,' Andre continued.

'To the three Bs,' Raf said.

They broke from the group hug and Andre turned the volume down on the stereo. 'So, I was thinking we should get our heads together and come up with some ideas for the Investor Showcase.'

'Get our heads together?' MJ looked confused.

'Talk about ideas,' Andre explained.

'Why don't we dance some ideas?' Raf said, playing with the beads around his neck.

'Yes, let's,' Billie said, smiling at him.

'OK. How 'bout we freestyle for a bit and see what happens?' Andre put 'Chimes' by Hudson Mohawke on and they all started to move.

As Tilly swayed to the beat she looked up at her graffiti art on the wall, and the three street-style bumblebees she'd painted. It had taken her ages to write the words in their speech bubbles, the Il Bello motto: *Be you. Be fearless. Be authentic.* She'd had to painstakingly copy each letter at a time so she didn't screw it up.

Pretty soon Raf and Billie were improvising some capoeira and contemporary moves, while Andre and MJ worked on some B-boy stalls and goofed around with some back and head spins, trying to land in a statuesque pose. But the more Tilly enjoyed their dancing, the more worried she became. What if she didn't get her academic grades up and her mum took her out of WEDA? How would she survive without Il Bello? At one point she was so distracted she whacked Andre in the head, mid-vogue. She was actually relieved when Andre called an end to the session, joking that he might need to add 'be non-violent' to their three Bs motto.

'You OK?' Andre asked as they made their way back to the dorm block.

Tilly nodded. She couldn't tell him what was

going on – as far as she was concerned, talking about your problems only made them a million times worse. And anyway, she didn't want Andre to think she was weak. She *wasn't* weak. She was a fearless flamingo. She would sort this out on her own. She watched as, way up ahead of them, Billie rushed down the gravel driveway to get her train home. Tilly felt a sad pang. It must be so nice for Billie to not have to worry about classes, or losing her place at WEDA.

As they got to the entrance to the dorms, Andre did a quick moonwalk along the low wall of the flowerbed outside. 'Fancy doing some work on Spotted tonight?' he asked, leaping back down in front of Tilly. 'I got some awesome photos when I was in New York.'

Tilly could think of nothing she'd rather do than help Andre with a blog post – but then she remembered the English homework she'd been set. 'Oh, Dre, I can't. I've got a homework emergency.'

'Already? We've only been back a day.'

'I know. But my English teacher's evil.' Tilly was too embarrassed to tell Andre the truth – that it would take her about ten times longer than anyone else to try to get it done.

Andre gave her a hug. 'All right – but you know where I am if you change your mind, Tillz.'

Tilly let herself into her room and sat down at her desk. Mrs Jarvis had asked them to write an account of their Christmas holidays, with a really strong opening paragraph. She turned on her laptop and stared at the blank screen. If only Mrs Jarvis had asked her to dance or paint how her holiday had been. She pictured herself voguing the loneliness and frustration she'd felt over Christmas under a spotlight in the front of class, and everyone completely understanding her. She groaned, realising that no matter how hard she tried, writing words would never help her express herself. She imagined painting a graffiti mural of her house, sliced open like a cake, each of her family members in their separate rooms – Bobby on his Xbox, her parents buried in work, and Tilly dancing in her bedroom, trying to break free. When she thought of expressing herself in these ways she felt a shiver of excitement. When she looked back at the screen, she felt a dull ache. Tilly sighed and shut her laptop. It was no good – her homework would have to wait.

She left her room and headed to the boys' corridor. Andre had stuck a handwritten sign on the door that read: *FASHION GURU AT WORK – DO NOT DISTURB!* Tilly grinned as she knocked.

Andre opened the door slightly and glared through the crack like he was about to yell at whoever had disturbed him. But when he saw that it was Tilly, his face broke into an answering grin and he flung the door wide open. 'You came!'

Tilly nodded. 'Homework can wait.'

'Amen, sweet-cheeks! Come in.'

As always, Andre's room smelled of vanilla

candles and his bed was covered with a jumbled mountain of clothes. By contrast, MJ's side of the room was immaculate. His bed was perfectly made, his desk was practically empty and there wasn't a single poster on his wall. Andre – who had covered his side with posters and photos and various fabric swatches – was itching to invade his wall space, but MJ wouldn't allow it.

'Where's MJ?' Tilly asked, sitting cross-legged on the floor.

'Library. He says he can't concentrate when I'm blogging – apparently I make too much noise.'

Tilly laughed. 'He has a point. You do tend to shriek a lot.'

'Huh! You'll be shrieking when you see what I spotted in Harlem.' Andre passed her his laptop. 'Is this not one of the fetchest outfits you have ever seen?'

'Wow!' Tilly looked at the selection of photos filling the screen. They were of a young woman, standing in front of a coffee shop. She was wearing a pretty standard leather jacket and woolly hat but the dress she was wearing stood out a mile: a knee-length fifties style that tapered in at the waist, made from a patchwork of different, brightly coloured material.

'Isn't it *awesome?*' Andre sat down next to Tilly, his eyes wide. 'But do you want to know the best bit? All of the patches were taken from clothes that once belonged to her grandmother. Listen to what she said . . .' Andre started reading from his phone. '"My grandma was my hero. She taught me to believe in myself and never stop trying. I made this dress so that I think of her every time I wear it. And I wear it every time I need to feel strong. Every patch holds a different memory – the pale blue one reminds me of the time we went to Nantucket for the weekend and she told me that I should chase my dream of becoming an artist. The rose pink one is from the dress she wore to my college graduation. The primrose yellow cotton is from the shirt she was wearing the last time I saw her before she died.

It reminds me of how precious life is and how I shouldn't waste a single day.'"

'Wowzers!' Tilly said.

'I know, right!' Andre put his phone down. 'What shall we call the blog post?'

Tilly looked back at the photos. She loved the power clothes had to express or change your mood, but this girl had taken it to a whole new level. 'How about, Dress of Dreams?'

'Yes!' Andre took his laptop from her and started typing.

'You should write about how fashion can make us fearless, how clothes aren't just for keeping us covered and warm but they can have meaning too.' Thoughts and ideas buzzed around Tilly's head. 'Like sometimes you want to wear something that will make you feel all cosy and safe, like – like fleecy pyjamas.'

'Speak for yourself,' Andre retorted.

'OK, I know a style icon like you wouldn't be seen dead in a pair of fleecy PJs, but most people need comfort clothes.'

'Ooh, comfort clothes – I like that.' Andre started typing again.

'And then other times, when you want to slay it, you put on your fearless clothes – no, your fearless fashion.'

'Fearless fashion,' Andre echoed as he typed.

'And then, when you need a little help believing in your dreams, you could create an outfit that inspires you – like that girl's dress of dreams.'

'Yes, yes, yes.' Andre carried on typing as Tilly spoke.

She felt like she was fizzing over now, bursting with ideas. 'Maybe we should set our readers a challenge? Get them to create an outfit that will help them to dream, like that dress!'

Andre stopped typing. 'Yes! And we could ask them to send photos in. We could get Bill to send one of her in that top you made. It's seriously fetch.'

'Thanks, bruh.' Tilly glowed with pride. 'I know . . . we could feature the best photos on our Fearless Fashion Board.'

Andre started typing again. 'This is awesome. You come up with the best ideas.'

'Do I?' Tilly's eyes widened in surprise as she looked at him. She'd felt so dumb for most of the day, it was weird receiving praise.

'Of course. You're an awesome blogger.' Andre moved the laptop closer to her. 'Now help me choose which photos to use.'

As Tilly looked through the photos she couldn't help sighing. If only she could feel this useful in her English lessons.

CHAPTER FIVE

The next morning, Tilly woke up extra early to try to get her English homework finished. Creating the new blog post for Spotted had given her a much-needed confidence boost. But as soon as she tried to translate her thoughts about her Christmas holiday into written words, her brain froze. It took so long to try to get the letters in the right order. It was so frustrating. Tilly's new buzz began draining fast. It took her half an hour to get one paragraph down and what she'd written sounded so dumb and boring. She felt anger rising inside of her, hot as fire. Dyslexia was like living inside a prison. All of the things she wanted to write just stayed trapped inside her head. She flung her notebook at her bed and it bounced off the wall with a clatter.

'What time is it?' Naomi muttered from beneath her duvet.

'Six-thirty,' Tilly replied.

'Drat!'

English was first period. When Tilly got to the classroom Billie was already there, with her homework assignment laid out in front of her. It was nearly two pages long. Tilly glanced across at Cassandra. She was sitting bolt upright, her hair scraped into a bun, her make-up and complexion flawless. She was holding an assignment that was pages long *and* included photos. Tilly thought of her hand-scrawled paragraph. It was going to look so lame compared to the others. Even though she hadn't had time for any breakfast, she felt sick to her stomach.

'Good morning, everyone,' Mrs Jarvis called as the rest of the class filed into the room. 'I hope you've all done your homework.'

Tilly's mouth went dry.

'Before you hand it in I thought it would be nice to hear some of your opening paragraphs to see how strong you made them.'

Tilly looked down at her notepad. Her opening paragraph was rubbish. And it was her only paragraph! She thought of having to read what she'd written in front of the class and she went red hot with embarrassment. *Think of something!* she silently pleaded with herself. Then, as one of the students at the front of the class started reading her work, the seed of an idea planted in Tilly's mind. What if she didn't read what she'd written at all? What if she pretended to read from her notepad but made something up as she went along like she did when she was helping Andre with his blog? Her ideas might flow more freely that way. As the students took it in turns to read their opening paragraphs, Tilly started searching her brain for words and ideas that summed up her holiday. They needed to be powerful. They needed to grab people's attention.

'Cassandra,' Mrs Jarvis called. 'Would you like to share next?'

Cassandra started reading about how 'super awesome' it had been to spend Christmas at some swanky ski resort. Tilly focused all of her attention on blocking her out. Free from having to write them down, ideas were starting to fill her mind. She just had to pray that they'd come out OK when it was her turn to speak.

'Thank you, Cassandra, that was lovely,' Mrs Jarvis said. 'Tilly, over to you.'

Tilly got to her feet and opened her notebook on a random page, holding it close, so no one else could see that she wasn't actually reading. *Just freestyle*, she told herself, *like you do when you're dancing. Let the words flow.*

'It was the worst of times . . . it was the worst of times,' she began, looking down at the blank page. 'And it should have been the best of times, the happiest of Christmas times. But my bedroom walls had turned to prison bars. And, like a vacant scroll through social media waiting for a like, I stared blankly at my screen, finding solace in an emoji, wishing that life was as simple as the smile I fake for a world that's never truly paying attention. You gave me your presents . . . but what I needed was your presence. A true smile to tell me that you see me, you believe in me. But – but all I got was judgement, wrapped up in scorn. My freedom's creative bubble . . . popped.'

Cassandra started coughing loudly, breaking Tilly's flow. She took a deep breath and looked at Mrs Jarvis anxiously. Her expression was impossible to read. Then Billie started clapping loudly, along with Raf and a few of the others.

'That was amazing!' Billie exclaimed.

'Really?' Tilly put her pad down and looked back at Mrs Jarvis.

'That was very powerful, Tilly,' Mrs Jarvis said with a smile. Finally, she'd made her smile! 'I can't wait to read the rest of it.'

Tilly's heart sank. How was she going to explain that there was no rest of it? That what she'd supposedly just read didn't actually exist.

'Why is your page blank?' Cassandra asked, leaning across the aisle and staring at Tilly's notebook.

'It's not,' Tilly snapped.

'Yes it is.' Cassandra sat back in her chair and folded her arms. 'You weren't reading at all just then. 'You were making it up.'

'I was . . . I – I wasn't!' Tilly stammered, her face flushing.

'Show me then,' Cassandra replied.

Tilly felt everyone's gaze burning into her. 'I – I don't have it on me.'

'Ha!' Cassandra exclaimed triumphantly. 'I knew you hadn't done it.'

'Shut up!' Tilly yelled.

'OK, that's enough,' Mrs Jarvis said. 'Tilly, have you or have you not done the homework?'

'I – I haven't written it down.'

Cassandra gave a haughty laugh. Tilly had to focus all of her energy on not going over and punching her.

'So, what did you just read?' Mrs Jarvis asked.

'It was some ideas I had – in my head.'

'Well, they were some very impressive ideas, Tilly, very impressive indeed,' Mrs Jarvis said. 'But I think you and I need to have a little chat after class about the importance of getting your homework finished in time. Meanwhile, Billie, would you like to read what you've written?'

As Billie started reading, Tilly felt frustration prickling beneath her skin. It didn't matter that Mrs Jarvis had liked her ideas. All that mattered was that they were written down. The one thing she couldn't do properly. She was never going to do well in this stupid class.

Mrs Jarvis was actually pretty nice about the whole homework situation when Tilly saw her after class, giving her until the weekend to get the assignment done and asking if she needed any help. Tilly had of course said no. If Cassandra found out she needed extra help to read and write, she'd make her life hell.

As soon as Tilly had managed to convince Mrs Jarvis that everything was OK and she'd have her homework done asap, she raced over to the new building for tap class. The rest of the class were all in position when she got to the studio. Mrs Jones frowned at her and looked pointedly at the clock on the wall.

'Sorry, I'm late, Miss, I had to stay behind to see my English teacher.'

'OK. But don't let it happen again.' Mrs Jones turned away to look for something in her bag.

Cassandra muttered something under her breath.

'What did you say?' Tilly whispered.

'Nothing,' Cassandra said, turning to smile sweetly at her. She looked like a Disney princess, but underneath she was frozen like an evil ice queen, Tilly knew that for sure.

'Just stay out of my business,' Tilly muttered.

'Oh my God, are you threatening me?' Cassandra said in a loud voice.

Mrs Jones turned to look at them. 'What's going on over there?'

'My dad doesn't donate thousands of pounds to WEDA for me to be threatened here,' Cassandra said, even louder.

'I didn't threaten you!' Tilly exclaimed.

'Enough!' Mrs Jones shouted, banging her cane on the floor.

Cassandra pouted. 'But she was –'

'I don't want to hear another word,' Mrs Jones said, walking over to them. 'Miss Murphy and I had quite enough of your squabbling last term and we're certainly not going to entertain another second of it this term. Do I make myself clear?'

'Yes, Mrs Jones,' Tilly murmured.

'Cassandra?' Mrs Jones rapped.

'Yes,' Cassandra muttered.

'Good. And as a way of helping you girls get over your differences I want you to dance together for the Investor Showcase.'

'*What?*' Cassandra looked horrified.

Tilly stared at Mrs Jones in disbelief.

'I'd like you to perform in the tap showcase.'

'But –' Tilly said.

'Professional dancers have to work together as a team,' Mrs Jones interrupted. 'No matter what their personal differences. This will be your chance to prove that you've got what it takes and that you deserve your places here at WEDA. Do you understand?'

The girls nodded.

'Good. Now let's get on with the class.'

'Oh my God, I can't believe Mrs Jones has done that to you!' Billie said to Tilly as they sat down in the canteen to eat lunch.

'I know. Just when I thought my day couldn't get any worse,' Tilly said glumly.

Billie placed her hand on top of Tilly's. 'I thought your piece in English was amazing.'

'Thank you. Shame Mrs Jarvis didn't.'

'But she did like it.'

'Yeah, until she found out I hadn't written it.' Tilly sighed and looked down at her soup. 'Now she wants me to write it down by the weekend.'

'I can help you.' Billie's eyes lit up. 'Why don't you come back to my house after school tomorrow? We can do it together.'

Tilly felt clammy with embarrassment. She hated the way she relied on Billie for help. It made her feel stupid and like some kind of charity case.

'You can sleep over. It'll be so much fun.' Billie took her phone from her bag. 'I'll call my mum and ask her.'

'But . . .' Tilly broke off. Billie looked so excited and it was really nice of her to offer to help. But Tilly couldn't help feeling a growing sense of dread. She couldn't keep relying on Billie. How was she going to manage in the exams? Tilly pushed her chair back. 'I'm going to go to the stable.'

Billie looked at her, confused. 'What? But I thought we weren't having a rehearsal this lunchtime.'

'We're not. Andre wants me to do another mural. I think I'll make a start.' Tilly stood up.

'Do you want me to help you?'

Tilly shook her head. She knew she'd be better

off being alone right now. 'No thanks, but I'll definitely come to yours tomorrow night.' She grabbed her bag and started walking to the door before Billie could say anything else.

Tilly let herself into the Stable Studio and turned on the lights. The blank wall glowed at her invitingly. She needed to paint something that would make her feel good about herself again. The image of a flamingo came into her mind – strong and bright and long-legged and proud. She popped a piece of gum into her mouth then she took her spray paints from her bag. As she began to spray-paint the black outline of a flamingo, she thought back to what had happened in English. For a brief moment she'd actually enjoyed the sensation of words flowing through her instead of being blocked. As she sprayed a long pair of flamingo legs, a new line popped into her head: *The spray of my paint releases me from this prison that I'm in.* She sighed and pushed the words from her mind. There was no point thinking about words – they only ever got her into trouble. She needed to switch off her brain and lose herself in her art. As she blew a bubble with her gum she had the idea to paint a huge pink bubble coming from the flamingo's mouth. The thought made her smile. And, slowly but surely, the tension that had been filling her body all morning began releasing itself with each spray.

CHAPTER
SIX

The first rehearsals for the Investor Showcase took place in the last lesson the following day. Mrs Jones had asked Tilly and Cassandra to meet her in the Murphy Studio to have a run-through of the dance she wanted them to perform. Tilly walked into the studio feeling dejected. Being paired with Cassandra meant they'd have to spend *hours* together rehearsing. She didn't know how they'd do it without killing each other. Cassandra was already in the studio, standing by the barre and talking to Mrs Jones. Pale gold sunlight was streaming in through the glass ceiling, pooling around Cassandra like a spotlight, making her skin glow and her hair shine. Tilly instinctively ran her finger over her face. She'd applied an extra layer of foundation in preparation for this moment but she could still feel the lumpy outline of the spots beneath. She wished she could scrape them off with a knife. Cassandra never seemed to get spots, or have a bad hair day. Like a Barbie doll fresh from the box, she was flawless every day.

'And my father said to tell you that he's very much looking forward to the Investor Showcase,' she said loudly, as Tilly walked over.

Tilly sighed. This was why there was no point even trying to fight Cassandra. Her dad contributed loads of money to WEDA, which Cassandra loved to remind them of at every opportunity.

'Ah, Tilly, there you are,' Mrs Jones said with a smile. 'I was just telling Cassandra that I've found the perfect piece for you both – the 'Duelling Banjos'. Hopefully it will provide a channel for the tension between you.' Mrs Jones looked at them both sternly. 'Now I don't know what's happened to cause this animosity and I don't want to know, but I will say this: students shouldn't feel the need to compete against each other. They should praise one another for their accomplishments and work together. You need to trust in each of your talents and abilities and realize that your differences make you stronger not weaker. Do I make myself clear?' She looked at Tilly and Cassandra.

Both girls nodded.

'Good. Now, in this routine you'll be working to your strengths and relying on each other's rhythms. You'll be drumming in-sync to bring the symphony of tap to this very impressive piece of music. There can be no underestimating the technical difficulties of this routine. It's also very funny. You'll both need to be fully focused to pull it off. There will be no time for petty squabbles. If you're going to get this right you'll have to pull together – for WEDA's sake and your own.'

'OK,' Tilly said. As much as she hated Cassandra, she loved WEDA way more and keeping her place in the academy was all that mattered.

'Right, let's work on a few rhythms.' Mrs Jones pointed with her cane to the middle of the studio floor. 'Begin with a cramp roll – starting slowly and speeding it up in time and in tune with each other until you can't go any faster – and then stop. It's up to you to decide when enough is enough, and you'll have to take the cue from each other without saying anything. You must read and respond to each other. If you over-compete you'll no longer be in time with one another, and avoiding that is the only way this piece will work.'

Tilly had been hoping that once they began she'd be able to lose herself and her insecurities in the dance, but they ended up becoming even worse. With her long legs and short hair, she felt so gangly and tomboyish next to Cassandra. And Cassandra's feet were stronger too, which meant she was able to do clearer, faster taps and more impressive rhythms. She could feel Cassandra's competitive edge forcing the tempo of their taps. By the end of the rehearsal Cassandra was beaming smugly and Tilly wanted to crawl into a corner and hide.

'Thank you so much for your efforts today,' Mrs Jones said, putting on her wrap. 'With your hard work and dedication, I think this routine is going to be one of the highlights of the showcase.'

As the girls left the studio, Cassandra turned to Tilly. 'Dancing with you is actually not nearly as bad as I thought it would be.'

'Oh?' Tilly looked at her warily. Was Cassandra trying to make up with her? Maybe she'd taken Mrs Jones's words to heart. Maybe this wasn't going to be so bad after all.

'Yes, you're the perfect partner to make me shine. You're really no competition at all.'

And, with a swish of her hair, Cassandra strode off down the hall.

I hate you, I hate you, I hate you! Tilly thought, fighting the urge to kick the wall.

*

Stomping her anger out along the way, Tilly went to her room to grab her overnight bag. When she checked her phone there was another text from her mum.

Jsut wonedring how yuor classes went taody.
Lte me know. Mum

'Aaaargh! Leave me alone!' Tilly yelled at the phone before stuffing it in her bag and hurrying to the main reception to meet Billie.

'How was the tap rehearsal?' Billie asked as soon as she saw her.

'Not great. Mrs Jones wants us to do a routine to the 'Duelling Banjos'.'

Billie stared at her. 'Isn't that the one where the dancers have a comedy battle?'

'Yep. Mrs Jones thinks it will help us to channel our hatred for each other into laughter. But I'm not so sure slapstick comedy in tap shoes is the answer . . . I think we might end up tapping each other to death!'

Billie laughed and linked her arm through Tilly's. 'Oh well, you can forget about all that for tonight at least. I can't wait for you to stay over. It's going to be super fun!'

Billie's flat was on a council estate on the outskirts of London. By the time the girls got there it was cold and dark. The air smelled of stale chips and a row of huge tower blocks loomed out of the darkness. Tilly pulled her coat closer around her. It must be so weird for Billie splitting her life between the magical world of WEDA and the estate. It was like being on two different planets. But stepping inside Billie's flat was like entering another world all over again. It was warm and cheery and smelled of baking.

'Hi, girls!' Billie's mum, Kate, said, coming into the hall to greet them. With her blond hair, green eyes and her wide, welcoming smile, she looked like Billie's older sister. 'It's so lovely to see you again, Tilly.'

'You too,' Tilly replied. 'I love your dress.'

Kate looked down at her lime-green sweater dress and smiled. 'Thank you. I wouldn't normally buy something so bright but Billie persuaded me to get it.'

'I was inspired by the "Bold is Beautiful" blog post you and Andre wrote on Spotted,' Billie explained.

'Seriously?' Tilly felt a fizz of excitement. It was mind-blowing to think that something she'd created could ripple like that.

She followed Billie and Kate into the kitchen. As they hugged, Tilly felt another wave of sadness and looked away. Her own mum wasn't a huggy person at all. The closest she came to physical affection was a pat on the shoulder. Tilly looked around the kitchen. It was so homely and bright, with the tiles on the wall forming a mosaic of red, orange, green and blue. A pot of something delicious-smelling was bubbling away on the stove and a tray of freshly baked cookies was cooling on the side. Tilly's eyes were drawn to a large noticeboard on the wall, framed with a string of fairy-lights and covered in a collage of pictures.

'That's our dream-board,' Billie said, coming over to Tilly. 'We put pictures of our dreams on it to try to help them come true. That's my side, with all the dancing pictures. Mum's is the side with all the pictures of cottages.'

'One day,' Kate said with a sigh.

'It's so cool!' Tilly said. She wondered what pictures she would put on a dream-board. An image of Cassandra falling, screaming, into the Grand Canyon popped into her head.

'I hope you girls are hungry,' Kate said. 'I've made a pot of chilli, and Tony's coming over later with dessert.'

'Tony is mum's new boyfriend,' Billie said with a grin. 'I think it's true luurrrrve.'

'Shut up,' Kate said, playfully nudging her in the ribs.

Tilly smiled but again felt a squeeze of sadness. She could never imagine being this relaxed with her mum. It must be so nice.

'How was your ballet class?' Kate asked Billie. 'Did you manage to do the quadruple turn with the leg thing you've been struggling with?'

Billie nodded. 'Yes, it was fine. I should have believed in myself a bit more!'

'That's great, honey. I'm so pleased.' Kate turned to stir the pot on the stove.

Tilly listened to them wistfully. Her own mum didn't know a pirouette from a plie. As Billie took a bite from one of the warm cookies and Kate playfully flicked a tea towel at her, Tilly's wistfulness soured into jealousy. She tried to push it down inside her, but it wasn't fair. Billie was a brilliant dancer, she did well in her academic subjects *and* she had a really fun and loving mum.

All through dinner, Tilly's feeling of jealousy bubbled away inside of her, making her feel even worse about herself. Billie and her mum were so nice – and so welcoming. She wanted to relax and have fun with them, but they kept reminding her of all the things she didn't have. And when Tony arrived with a strawberry cheesecake it got even worse. He was so friendly and jolly and nice. They were like the perfect family.

'Who fancies a game of Scrabble?' Tony asked once they'd finished eating.

Tilly's heart sank. Scrabble, with all of its letters and words, was her worst game ever. He might as well have said, 'Who wants to have all their teeth pulled out?'

Luckily, Billie seemed to sense how she was feeling. 'We've got homework to do,' she said, getting to her feet.

'Oh, what a shame,' Kate said. 'Scrabble with Tony is so much fun.'

'He's always inventing new words,' Billie explained.

'I'm not,' Tony replied with a grin. 'I just have a huuuuuge vocabulary!'

'Hmm, a huge imagination, more like,' Kate said with a giggle.

As Tilly followed Billie through to her bedroom

she felt really bad. Billie had already done her English homework. Now a fun night was being ruined because she had to help Tilly with hers.

'Shall we make a start?' Billie said, fetching her laptop from her desk.

'OK...' Tilly's skin prickled with embarrassment. It felt as if Billie was her mum and she was a five-year-old kid. She didn't want to be helped with her homework but she had no choice. As she sat down on Billie's bed she noticed a black and white photo of a man holding a little girl on Billie's bedside cabinet. From her wavy blond hair Tilly guessed that the girl must be Billie. And the man had to be her dad. Billie didn't talk about her dad much but Tilly knew that he'd died years ago and that Billie had started going to ballet lessons as a way of getting over her grief. She felt a wave of guilt for being resentful of Billie. It must have been horrible losing her dad when she was so young.

'Have you ever thought about asking for help with your dyslexia?' Billie said, as she sat down next to Tilly.

'What do you mean?'

'At WEDA. Maybe there's something the teachers can do to make things easier for you – like give you extra time to get things done.'

Tilly thought of how she'd been given extra time for certain assignments in her last school – and how some of the other kids had made fun of her for it. She didn't ever want to go back to that again. It was like having a neon sign over her head saying *STUPID*.

'I don't need extra time,' she muttered. Then a horrible thought occurred to her. Was Billie suggesting this because she was fed up of helping her? Was she tired of having to read things out or write things down? 'You don't have to help me, you know.'

'What do you mean?' Billie looked at her, confused. 'I want to help you.'

But Tilly wasn't able to control the embarrassment she was feeling. 'I don't need your help. I don't need anyone's help!' she snapped, her face burning. Just then, her phone bleeped. She took it from her pocket, hoping it was Andre sending one of his usual hilariously sarcastic messages. But the text was from her mum. Tilly's heart sank as she read it.

Yuor dad and I aer going to be pasisng WEDA on Sundya on the way bcak from dropipng Bobby at uni so we thuohgt we'd sotp by and taek you to lnuch. Mum

Tilly stared at the text until she was able to decipher enough words to work out what it meant. WEDA. Sunday. Lunch. Her heart sank. That was all she needed. Another grilling about how she was doing at school. She turned her phone off, then faked a yawn.

'Would it be OK if we went to sleep?' she asked Billie. 'I'm feeling really tired.'

The disappointment on Billie's face made Tilly's heart hurt, but she just couldn't face any more talk about how stupid she was.

'But it's still so early, Tillz!'

'I know. I'm sorry. I think I overdid it in tap.'

Tilly felt sick. This was not how she'd wanted the night to go at all but she couldn't help it.

'OK.' Billie put her laptop back on her desk and took a pair of pyjamas out from under her pillow. 'I'll go and brush my teeth.'

As soon as she'd left the room Tilly got into her pyjamas and slipped under the duvet on the spare bed. When she heard Billie coming back in she closed her eyes.

'Tilly?' Billie whispered.

'Yes,' Tilly murmured, pretending to be half-asleep.

There was a pause. 'It doesn't matter. Good night.'

'Night, Bill.' Tilly kept her eyes closed until she heard the click of the light being turned off and Billie getting into bed. Then she stared up into the darkness, tears rolling down her face.

CHAPTER SEVEN

'I'm staging an intervention!' Andre declared as he marched into Tilly's dorm room on Saturday morning and flung open the curtains.

Tilly looked up from her laptop, where she'd been painstakingly typing up her English homework, and frowned. 'I don't get you.'

'Get that you've been walking around looking like the misery emoji for the past few days, so I'm here to turn that frown upside down, and help you feel fearless again, sweetie! Get dressed, we're going out.'

'I am dressed.'

Andre tilted his head to one side and pursed his lips. 'No, you're not.'

Tilly looked at her tracksuit. When she'd got

up this morning all she could think about was her homework. She'd pulled on the first thing she saw. 'What's wrong with what I'm wearing? And where are we going?'

'Everything. And Camden.'

'Everything?'

'It's blue. Blue tracksuits are so last century.' Andre walked over to her wardrobe and started pulling out clothes.

Tilly shuddered. 'Oh no, I'm turning into one of those tragic people.'

'What tragic people?' Andre looked at her over his shoulder.

'Those tragic people who don't care what they wear. Who trudge around in tracksuits all day and say things like, "Isn't Velcro a great invention?"'

'Over my dead body you are.' Andre turned back to rummage in her wardrobe. 'Where's Dratzilla?' He nodded towards Naomi's bed.

'Gone to her grandma's for the weekend with Jordan.'

'Excellent!' Andre went over to Naomi's chair and picked up the scarf draped over one of the arms. 'I've had my eye on this scarf since last term.' He wrapped it around his neck and went over to the mirror. 'I knew it. It suits me perfectly.'

'Dre, you can't just take it.'

'Why not?' Andre glared at her. 'It goes perfectly with this bomber jacket.'

He was right, but that didn't justify blatant theft. Tilly frowned at him. 'She'll think I took it, you fashion criminal.'

'I'm not going to keep it. I'm just going to wear it today. She'll never know it was gone.' Andre threw a pair of tartan leggings and a black hoodie over to Tilly. 'Quick. Put these on – with your biker jacket and Docs. Maybe they'll reboot your personality, too. The next train to London's in twenty minutes.'

All the way up to Camden, Andre entertained Tilly with stories of fashion disasters he'd spotted in New York. It was so nice to get out of WEDA and forget about her mountain of homework for a while.

'I'm thinking we need to do something different on the blog,' Andre said, as their train pulled into Camden station.

'Like what?'

Andre pursed his lips, the way he always did when he wasn't sure about something. 'I don't know. But I'll know it when I see it.'

Even though it was January, Camden High Street bustled with tourists.

'Tourist fashion is so basic,' Andre said with a sigh. 'All those anoraks and stone-washed jeans. They make my Inner Fashionista want to wail.'

'Don't worry, I'm sure it won't be wailing for long. Look at that punk!' Tilly nodded at a guy who was browsing through a rail of T-shirts outside a shop. His ears, nose and lips were covered with piercings and his dark purple hair was gelled into a huge Mohican.

'Holy nose-bolts!' Andre whispered. 'He looks fierce.'

Tilly grinned. 'I wish I could get a nose piercing.'

Andre looked at her excitedly. 'You should! There must be somewhere up here you could get it done. This place must be the piercing capital of the world.'

Tilly shook her head. 'My parents are taking me out to lunch tomorrow. I don't think a nose piercing would go down too well.'

'So what? It's your nose, girl.'

'Not as far as my mum's concerned.'

'Parents.' Andre linked arms with her and slowly they made their way down the high street to Camden Market. The market was Tilly's favourite place in all of London. She loved the little tunnels and alcoves and all the crazy market stalls, with their wafting smells of incense. She loved the chatter and the laughter and the mixture of accents, and how it seemed like the whole world was there. As they browsed the clothes stalls and the jewellery and the art, they paused to take photos of anything that inspired them – a look, a colour scheme, an unusual combination. Anything that could be used on a future Spotted post. Finally, they emerged from the market, out on to the lock.

'Oh my God!' Andre exclaimed. 'The food smells divine!'

Tilly looked at all the food stalls, her stomach rumbling. She hadn't had much of an appetite all week as she'd been so stressed about her school work, but now it was back with a vengeance.

'Shall we get some lunch?' Andre asked.

'Yes!'

They started weaving their way between the stalls, stopping at one of them to buy cups of warm apple juice spiced with cinnamon and cloves. Tilly smiled as the warmth from the cup thawed her icy fingers. They walked a little further into the food market, past a burger stall and a pizza stand and a truck selling Thai street food.

'It all smells so good!' Andre groaned. 'How

are we ever going to decide?'

Tilly noticed a stall with a brightly painted banner saying *DUCKLICIOUS*. A Chinese man was standing behind it, making crispy duck pancakes. 'How about that one?' she said, pointing to the stall, practically drooling.

'Duck?' Andre looked horrified. 'We can't eat duck!'

'Why not?'

'Because I'm a ducketarian! Ducks are way too cute to eat.'

Tilly frowned at him. 'But you eat other animals.'

'I know, but other animals aren't as cute as ducks.'

'Pigs are pretty cute,' Tilly said. 'And cows. And what about lambs? They're super cute.'

'Oh my God!' Andre clapped his hand to his mouth, horrified. 'You're right. All animals *are* cute. I can't believe I've been so blinkered, just avoiding duck.' He looked around the market and stood bolt upright. 'I hereby declare myself vegan!'

'Vegan?' Tilly stared at him. 'But isn't that where you can only eat seeds?'

Andre frowned. 'Of course not. Vegans can eat loads of things . . . they can eat nuts and vegetables and . . .' He tailed off, looking slightly dejected.

Tilly frowned. 'Exactly.'

'Well, you keep eating your poor, defenceless animals. I'm off to find some nuts.' Andre started stalking back through the food market.

Tilly's heart sank as she followed him past all the delicious-smelling stalls until finally they arrived at a truck called The Veggie Van, which was covered in cartoon-style paintings of vegetables with smiling faces.

'Here we go,' Andre said. 'This looks perfect.' He turned to Tilly. 'Think how much happier you'll be not having a crispy duck massacre on your conscience.'

Tilly sighed and took her purse from her bag. They both ordered something called falafel, which came in a wrap, then went and sat over by the lock.

'Mmm, delicious,' Andre said loudly as he took a bite. But Tilly couldn't help noticing him glancing wistfully at the burger stand.

'So, what's up, Tillz?' Andre asked, when they were halfway through their lunch.

'Nothing.' Tilly looked away, to a young guy busking by the entrance to the market.

'Come on. You've been acting like a total stress-head ever since we got back from Christmas break. What is it?'

'I'm just worried about what my mum said – about her taking me out of WEDA.'

'But that isn't going to happen, is it?' Andre looked at her, his dark brown eyes wide with concern. 'All you have to do is get your grades up.'

Tilly sighed. If only it were that easy.

'You will be able to get your grades up, won't you?' Andre stuffed the remainder of his falafel back in its paper bag.

'Yes. Of course. It just means I need to work a bit harder, that's all.'

'Good. Cos we've all been worried about you. Especially Billie.'

Tilly's face flushed. Had Billie told him what had happened at their sleepover?

'Why? What did she say?'

'Whoa! Easy, tiger. She just said she was worried about you – that you seemed a little stressed.'

'Well, she's got no reason to be worried. I'm fine,' Tilly said.

'OK. Good.' Andre didn't exactly look convinced.

'So, have you got any ideas for Spotted yet?' Tilly asked, desperate to change the subject.

Andre sighed. 'No, not yet, unless . . .' He looked down at the Veggie Van bag in his lap. 'OMG, I think I've got something.'

'What?' Tilly looked at him excitedly.

'Let's do a vegan post!'

'A vegan post?' Tilly frowned. 'What, about food?'

'No! About fashion. Fashion that's fabulous and flash, with a conscience.'

'But I don't get what being vegan has to do with clothes.'

Andre jumped to his feet. 'Being vegan has *everything* to do with clothes. Come on, I'll show you.'

Tilly followed Andre back into the market.

'Now where was it?' Andre muttered as he led her through one of the tunnels. 'Ah yes, here it is.' He turned to Tilly triumphantly. 'Look.'

Tilly followed his gaze to a stall selling shoes. The sign above it read VEGAN FOOTWEAR. The image of a load of shoes eating vegetables popped into Tilly's mind and she couldn't help smiling.

'I can assure you that fabulous footwear with a conscience is nothing to smile about,' Andre snapped before pursing his lips. 'Well, actually, I suppose it is – as long as you're not smiling because you're mocking it.'

'Of course I'm not mocking it. I just don't get how a pair of shoes can be vegan.'

Andre raised his perfectly arched eyebrows and gave a dramatic sigh. 'It's not about diet, it's about what they're made from.'

'What? They're made from vegetables?' Tilly stared at the shoes. They all looked pretty normal to her.

'Oh my God, no! It means they're not made from leather. You know, as in the skin of a cow.'

'Oh, I seeeeee.'

'Let's find a pair we can feature on Spotted.' Andre started scanning the stall until he found a pair of bright red men's brogues. 'I'm getting all of the tingles,' he said, passing the shoes to Tilly. 'What do you reckon?'

As Tilly looked at the shoes her skin started tingling too. They were so bright and cheery. And so beautifully made. 'Yep. They pass the test.'

The shoes were also hugely expensive so, while Tilly distracted the stall-holder, Andre took a couple of quick photos of them, then popped them back on their stand.

Then, after trawling the market for other examples of fabulous fashion with a conscience, they went back outside to the lock and loaded the photos to the blog.

'I feel just like Jesus,' Andre said as he pressed publish.

'What? Why?' Tilly stared at him.

'Using my position to help others. Standing up for the poor defenceless animals . . . and the ducks. Promoting fashion with a conscience.'

Tilly started to giggle. And once she started she couldn't stop.

'What? Why are you laughing?'

But Andre's indignant expression only made her laugh harder, until tears were rolling down her face. 'Oh, Dre, thank you!'

'What for?'

'Making me laugh.'

Andre frowned. 'It wasn't supposed to be a joke.'

'I know . . . that makes it funnier!'

Andre sighed. 'Are you saying I'm not like Jesus?'

Tilly nodded. 'Not really. I mean, Jesus didn't exactly have a fashion blog.'

Andre sighed again. 'How about Lady Gaga then? You can't deny she's fabulousness with a conscience.

She's always using her position to promote a good cause.' Andre stood upright and stared into the distance. 'When facing life's challenges, always ask yourself, "What would Gaga do?" and do more of that. Long live The Ga!' Andre stood to attention, pushed his hip out and gave a salute.

'Yep, you're way more like Lady Gaga than Jesus.' Tilly leaned against Andre and rested her head upon his shoulder, so grateful for her crazy, hilarious friend.

CHAPTER EIGHT

Tilly woke up bright and early on Sunday morning and finished her English homework. She'd tried writing up what she'd said in class, but had got tangled up in typos and none of it made any sense. So, in the end, she'd resorted to listing all the things she'd done over the break: Christmas shopping, Christmas dinner, customizing the captain's hat, seeing her brother. There was no way her assignment was as good as Billie's or Cassandra's and, at just under a page, it certainly wasn't as long, but at least it was done. Her day out with Andre had left her feeling hopeful again – though she had had to wrestle Naomi's scarf back from him at the end of the day – and that hope had energized her. It had even made her feel slightly more positive about lunch with her mum.

Tilly got changed into the most sensible dress in her wardrobe – a faded denim shirt dress – and applied the lightest layer of foundation. She looked in the mirror and tried not to flinch at the dullness of her reflection. 'Don't worry, fearless flamingo,' she whispered. 'I'll let you out again later, I promise.' She was determined not to do anything to upset her mum today.

On her way down to the main entrance to meet her parents she bumped into MJ, who was sitting on one of the plush leather sofas in reception, reading a book. MJ often hung out there at the weekends, on his own. At first Tilly had worried that he was lonely, but she'd come to realize that he liked the peace and quiet of the main building without the other students around. For MJ, being alone wasn't something to be feared, it was a refuge. She could relate to that.

'Hey,' she said softly, as she walked over to him.

MJ looked up and nodded. 'Hey,' he said, without smiling.

At first, Tilly had taken MJ's abruptness as a sign of unfriendliness but now she really liked it about him. He was just super honest.

'I'm off out to lunch with my parents,' she said. 'Wish me luck.'

'Why?' MJ looked at her over the top of his book.

'Why am I going to lunch with them?'

MJ shook his head. 'No, why should I wish you luck?'

'Oh. Because my mum likes to give me a tough time about my school work.'

'Why?'

'Because I'm not doing so well academically.' It was weird. When she was with Billie or Andre or any of the others, Tilly hated admitting that she found her school work hard, but with MJ she didn't feel embarrassed at all.

'I'm sorry to hear that. Let me know if I can help you with anything.'

'Thanks, MJ.' Tilly smiled but he'd already disappeared back behind his book. 'I'll see you later.'

'Maybe.'

Tilly made her way out on to the gravel driveway. Her parents were already there, waiting in the car. She ran over and got into the back seat.

'Hi!' she said, as cheerily as she could.

'What have you done to your hair?' her mum asked, turning to look at her from the front passenger seat.

Tilly's heart sank. 'I dyed it red.'

'Well, I can see that. But why?'

'Because I wanted to.' Tilly put her seatbelt on, her heart sinking. This was going to be a long lunch.

'And your teachers allowed it?'

'Yes. They like us expressing ourselves through our appearance.'

Her mum gave a heavy sigh.

Tilly's stomach churned. They hadn't even left yet and it was already going horribly wrong.

'Well, I think it looks very nice, love,' Tilly's dad said, starting the car.

'Thanks, Dad.' Tilly gazed out of the window gloomily as they drove from the academy grounds. *You're only going for lunch*, she reminded herself. *You will be coming back here later.* But how long for? All the fears that she'd managed to get under control the day before started nipping away at her again.

Her parents took her to a restaurant in a picturesque village close to WEDA. It was the kind of restaurant that liked to pretend it was still the olden days, with wooden beams, antique artefacts dotted around the place and old black and white photos on the walls. Tilly sat down at the table opposite her mum and dad and pretended to be fascinated by the menu. Really, she was just trying to avoid having to talk to them.

'So, how's it going back at WEDA?' her dad asked.

'Really good.'

'And how are you getting on in your classes?' her mum asked.

'Great.' The lie slipped out before Tilly had a chance to stop it.

'Really?' Her mum's frown faded.

'Yeah. I – uh – I got a really good mark for my English homework this week.'

'That's fantastic,' her dad said, with a beaming smile.

'What was it on?' her mum asked, not looking entirely convinced.

'We had to write an account of our Christmas holidays with a really strong opening paragraph,' Tilly replied, thankful that this, at least, was not a lie.

'And what grade did you get?' her mum asked.

'B – B plus,' Tilly said, looking back at her menu, hoping they wouldn't see her face flushing.

'Well done.' Her mum's voice was soft now, the way it was when she spoke to Bobby. Tilly glanced up and saw that she was smiling. It made her feel warm inside.

'I'm doing well in my other subjects too,' she said quickly. 'I'm trying really hard.'

'Excellent,' her mum said, her smile growing. 'I can't wait to hear how you do in your Maths test next week.'

Tilly stared at her. 'What Maths test?'

'I rang and spoke to the Head of Dance and Wellness at the beginning of the week. What's her name again?'

'Miss Murphy,' Tilly replied numbly.

'Yes. I told her how concerned I'd been at your end-of-term results and asked her if there was any way I could keep an eye on how you're doing. She told me you've got a Maths test next week and she'd email the result to me.'

Tilly forced herself to smile. 'Oh.'

For the rest of lunch it felt as if Tilly had been split in two. While her body sat and ate and chatted to her parents, her mind went nuts, panicking about what to do. She was terrible at Maths. And she was even worse in a Maths test, where she couldn't refer to her books or look up what the questions meant online. If she did badly her mum might get suspicious about her other subjects. What if she found out she'd lied about her English grade? What if she found out she hadn't even got her homework in on time?

By the time her parents dropped her back at WEDA, a couple of hours later, Tilly was jittery with anxiety. As she walked into reception she saw MJ still there on the sofa, lost in his book.

'Hey, MJ,' she said softly.

'Hey. How did your lunch go?'

'Don't ask.'

'Why not?' MJ put his book down.

'It didn't go well.'

MJ frowned. 'When things don't go well I like to dance.'

'Me too,' Tilly agreed.

MJ stood up. 'Why don't we then?'

'What, dance?'

'Yes.'

'Where?'

'Here, of course.'

Tilly looked around the deserted reception area. 'What would we dance to?'

MJ took his phone from his pocket. 'I've got the perfect track.'

The opening chords of Michael Jackson's 'Bad' rang out around the reception and Tilly couldn't help grinning. She might have known MJ would choose a song by his hero. She watched as MJ loosened his body into the groove. Then he spun around, threw his fedora into the air and deftly side-stepped so it landed back on his head.

'Come on,' he said, holding his hand out to Tilly.

At first, Tilly felt self-conscious, dancing in the reception. But not for long. Soon Doctor Dance had worked its magic and she was completely lost in the rhythm. She followed MJ over to the reception desk and next thing she knew, they were both standing on top of it, tapping out a rhythm on the shiny wood. Then they leaped off the desk and freestyled around the coffee table and between the sofas. MJ moonwalked and Tilly vogued, and with every pose she felt her anxiety fading. As the song came to an end they collapsed in a breathless heap on one of the sofas.

'Better?' MJ asked.

Tilly nodded. 'Loads. Thank you.'

'You're welcome.' MJ picked up his phone and his book. 'I'm going to get some dinner. Are you coming?'

Tilly shook her head. 'No. I have some work to do – I'll grab something later.'

'OK.'

While MJ set off for the canteen, Tilly made her way back to her room. Naomi still wasn't back yet. Tilly turned on the light and went over to her desk. She took out her Maths book. Maths was supposed to be about numbers but it involved so many words, especially in a test. The questions were full of them. Words like 'multiply' and 'divide' and 'fraction' and 'calculate'. Tilly found it so hard to remember what these words were, let alone what they meant. But she was going to have to figure it out somehow. She was going to have to do well in her test. She put on her pink crystal headphones and searched her playlist for Twenty One Pilots. Their music always made her feel chilled. Then she opened her Maths book and set to work.

CHAPTER NINE

'Put down your pancake, I have something to show you. Something *way* more important than food!'

Tilly looked up from her breakfast to see Andre standing on the other side of the table, holding his laptop.

'Dre, nothing is way more important than a blueberry pancake,' Tilly replied.

'Er, yes it is.' Andre sat down and placed his laptop in front of her. 'Look at these comments we've been getting.'

Tilly looked at the screen. Their Dress of Dreams post had got over fifty new comments. She started scrolling through them, wide-eyed. Loads of their readers had taken the challenge and created outfits that made them feel fierce or inspired them to dream. Most of them had posted photos of their outfits too.

'Whooooa!' Tilly tingled with excitement as she read. The comments were all so nice. They were so grateful to Spotted for daring them to be more creative with their look.

Andre grinned. 'Who needs *Vogue* when you've got Spotted? OMG, do you think Anna Wintour will hear about this and get in touch?'

Tilly laughed. 'Somehow I think she might be a little bit too busy being in charge of, like, the entire fashion world.'

Andre shrugged. 'Whatevs! So, I was thinking . . .' Andre grabbed a couple of blueberries from Tilly's pancake. 'We should make "fabulous and fierce" the theme of the Il Bello look for the Investor Showcase.'

Tilly nodded, although with all the pressure she was under from her academic subjects and performing the tap routine with Cassandra, she'd barely given Il Bello's performance a second thought.

'Let's talk to the others about it at lunch,' Andre said. 'But in the meantime, get your bejewelled and fabulous thinking cap on. Let's see if we can come up with some ideas for outfits for the others.'

Tilly nodded, but she felt her stomach clench. There were so many things on her mind right now, there didn't seem to be room for anything else.

Andre stood up. 'OK. Gotta go iron my new pinstripe waistcoat. Wait till you see it. It's fetch with a capital F, E, T, C and H!'

The first lesson of the day was English.

'Thank you, Tilly.' Mrs Jarvis smiled as Tilly handed her homework over. 'I'm really looking forward to reading this after the taster you gave us the other day.'

Tilly's heart sank. What she'd ended up writing was nothing like what she'd said in class. She hoped Mrs Jarvis wouldn't be too disappointed. She went and sat down next to Billie.

Cassandra leaned across the aisle towards her.

As always, her glossy hair framed her flawless skin. 'Did I just witness a miracle? Did you actually just hand in a piece of homework?'

'Shut up!' Tilly muttered. She quickly pictured Cassandra being eaten by a fire-breathing dragon to make herself feel better.

'Just ignore her,' Billie said, taking her books from her bag and placing them on the table. 'How was your weekend? Did you do anything fun?'

'I went to Camden with Andre, to get some photos for the blog.' Tilly hung her leather jacket on the back of her chair. 'And yesterday my parents took me for lunch.'

'That's nice,' Billie replied.

Tilly stifled a sigh. In Billie's world a family lunch would be nice – it would involve fun and laughter and hugs; a mum who really got you and a stepdad who made everyone laugh with his huuuuuge vocabulary.

'OK, everyone, settle down,' Mrs Jarvis called, picking up a pile of papers from her desk. 'I have your marked homework assignments for you.' She stood up and started handing out the assignments. 'I have to say, I was extremely impressed with what you've done. Some of the opening paragraphs were wonderful.'

Mrs Jarvis came over to Billie and handed over her homework. 'Excellent job, Billie. Really well written.'

Tilly glanced down at the paper. There was an A-star written in red at the top. Tilly felt a sour twinge of jealousy swiftly followed by guilt. Billie was such a lovely person. It wasn't her fault if English came easy to her. Tilly felt like a terrible friend for feeling resentful.

'And Cassandra,' Mrs Jarvis said, walking across the aisle. 'Yours is excellent too. Keep up the good work.'

'Oh, I will, Mrs Jarvis,' Cassandra said smugly.

Tilly kept her eyes fixed firmly on her desk. It was bad enough having to hear Cassandra gloating, there was no way she wanted to see it, too.

For most of the rest of the lesson, Mrs Jarvis got

them to read the first couple of chapters of the book they were studying that term.

Tilly focused hard on the dancing letters, trying to get them into an order she could understand. She felt a burst of happiness as she actually figured out the first couple of sentences. But her happiness soon faded when she realized that Billie was already on the third page. She started turning the pages in time with the rest of the class, pretending to read, all the while hoping that Mrs Jarvis didn't ask them about it at the end.

Thankfully, Mrs Jarvis didn't ask them any questions – but when the bell rang for the end of class she came over to Tilly with her homework.

'I managed to mark this while you were all reading,' she said. 'I was disappointed not to see any of the things you said in class last week.'

Although all the other students were getting ready to go, Tilly noticed Billie and Cassandra both watching. Mrs Jarvis placed the piece of paper on the desk. She'd written a big red D at the top.

Tilly's eyes smarted and she blinked hard. D for disappointment. D for dumb.

'Never mind,' Billie said, placing her hand on Tilly's arm. 'It's only one assignment.'

Tilly shook her hand off. It wasn't only one assignment. It was every assignment. Words were never going to make any sense to her. She was never going to get her grades up.

'Let me help you next time,' Billie whispered.

'I don't need your help!' Tilly snapped. She grabbed her books and stuffed them in her bag. Then she headed for the door.

Of course the next lesson had to be a tap rehearsal with Cassandra. Tilly raced to the girls' toilets and pulled out her make-up bag. She couldn't face Cassandra while feeling so bad about herself. She needed to do something to make herself feel stronger. She put some fresh concealer on her spots and reapplied her eyeliner. 'You can do this,' she whispered to her reflection. 'Don't let her get to you.' Then she hurried to the studio, determined not to be late again.

When she got there Cassandra was warming up by the barre but there was no sign of Mrs Jones.

'I don't know why Billie bothers being friends with you,' Cassandra said, as Tilly came over and put her bag down. 'You have nothing in common.'

'Yes we do. And anyway, friends don't have to have everything in common,' Tilly replied. *Just ignore her*, she told herself as she started doing some leg stretches. *Don't get sucked into an argument.*

'But she's so much cleverer than you,' Cassandra said, pulling her body into a perfect arabesque cascading into a giant penche. 'It must be so boring for her.'

'Shut *up*,' Tilly muttered. She pictured Cassandra at the top of a mountain, tripping on a rock and tumbling to her doom.

'But it's true – she is cleverer. I don't know how she can be bothered to hang out with you.'

'I said, *shut up!*' Tilly nudged Cassandra, sending her toppling to one side.

'Tilly!'

Tilly froze at the sound of Mrs Jones's voice. She turned and saw her standing in the doorway, holding her cane and glaring.

'I'm sorry, Mrs Jones, I –'

'Come here, now.' Mrs Jones beckoned to her.

Tilly trudged over to the door. She didn't need eyes in the back of her head to know that Cassandra would be gloating – again!

'What is going on with you?' Mrs Jones said.

'Nothing, I –'

'I meant what I said the other day, about dancers having to work together as a team.'

'I know. I just . . .' Tilly stood, head bowed. What could she say? 'I promise it won't happen again.'

'Good. Being here is an honour. I need to know that you appreciate it and that you're prepared to work for the good of the academy.'

'I do!'

'I'm glad. Now show me how much.' She gestured to the studio.

Tilly walked back over to Cassandra, face burning.

At lunchtime when Tilly got to the stable the rest of the crew were already waiting.

'Here she is!' Andre exclaimed. 'Come on then, tell us your ideas, Tillz.'

Tilly stared at him blankly. 'What ideas?'

'Our outfits for the show?'

'Oh.' Tilly's heart sank as all of Il Bello smiled at her expectantly. 'I'm sorry. I didn't get a chance.'

'Oh.' Andre's look of disappointment was crushing. 'Never mind, we can have a think tonight.'

'I can't tonight,' Tilly said, feeling horrible. 'I have a Maths test tomorrow.'

'We all have a Maths test in our classes tomorrow,' Andre replied. 'It's not a big deal. It's only to see how we're doing. I'm not doing any revision for it. Are any of you guys?'

The others all shook their heads.

You don't need to do any! Tilly wanted to scream. *But I do. Because I'm Dumb and Disappointing with a capital D.* She felt tears beginning to burn in the corners of her eyes. She had to get out of there before she made a total fool of herself.

'I'm not feeling too good,' she muttered. 'I think I'll go to my room for the rest of lunch.'

'What's wrong, babe?' Andre immediately looked concerned.

'Do you need some water?' Raf offered her his bottle.

Tilly shook her head.

'Can I get you anything?' Billie asked. She looked really worried too. Billie was so kind to Tilly but all she felt in return was resentment. Cassandra was right – she didn't deserve Billie as a friend. She didn't deserve any of Il Bello.

'I'm fine. I just need to be alone,' she snapped, before rushing to the door.

When she got back to her room she flung herself on her bed and stared up at the ceiling.

'What am I go to do?' she wailed.

Her phone buzzed. She took it from her pocket,

thinking it might be a message from Andre or Billie, but it was her mum.

Godo lukc in yuor maths test tormorow! Mum

'Aaaargh!' Tilly started pacing up and down the room. Although her mum's text sounded nice and supportive, she knew it was really a threat. That her mum was really saying, 'You'd better do well or else.'

Tilly stared at her reflection in the mirror on the door. 'Come on! Think of something!'

And then a thought popped into her head that made her feel sick with nerves and tingly with hope at the same time. No one else was going to be able to help her in this stupid test, so she'd just have to help herself. She sat down at her desk and took an index card from the drawer. She was going to have to cheat.

CHAPTER TEN

The next day, Tilly made her way to the Maths class feeling sick to the pit of her stomach. She hated what she was about to do but she had no choice. She couldn't lose her place at WEDA. She had to get a good mark in this test. She put her hands into the pocket of her hoodie and felt the sharp edges of the index card she'd hidden there.

'Are you OK, Tillz?' Billie asked, rushing over to Tilly as soon as she walked in.

Tilly nodded. She hadn't seen Billie since the day before, when she'd run from the stable – she'd ended up taking the afternoon off sick. 'Yeah, I'm fine, Bill.' It came out a lot sharper than Tilly had intended, and Billie turned away, looking hurt.

But Tilly couldn't worry about Billie's feelings now, she had to stay focused on getting through this test.

'OK, guys, get a wriggle on,' Mr Brown, their Maths teacher called from the front of the class. Mr Brown was one of those super-smiley teachers who said words like 'guys' and 'awesome'. Normally Tilly liked him, but today it felt as if he was the evil-doer who could be responsible for her leaving WEDA. She looked at the pile of test papers he was holding and her stomach churned. In her dorm room last night she'd practised getting the card from her pocket without being seen. She'd gone through all her clothes until she decided on a tatty hoodie with a faded picture of a pink Care Bear and a rainbow on the front. Andre had practically had a heart attack when he'd seen her in it at breakfast. But the baggy, fraying sleeves were perfect for slipping a card into. She stuffed her hands back into her pocket and slid the card up one of her sleeves. That part was easy. But how was she going to read from the card without being noticed? When she'd taken it out in her dorm room, the movement had seemed really discreet. But now, under the harsh glare of the lights and surrounded by all of her classmates, she wasn't so sure.

'OK, guys, quiet, please.' Mr Brown started walking around the class, putting test papers on each of the desks.

Tilly felt her throat tighten. If only she'd brought a bottle of water. Why hadn't she brought a bottle of water? Panic started rising inside her. Maybe she wouldn't need the card, she told herself. Maybe the questions would be simple and she'd be able to work out what they meant. Inside her hoodie pocket she slid the card back out from her sleeve and placed her hands on the desk. She might be panicking over nothing. Mr Brown placed a test paper in front of her, face down. The moment of truth was just seconds away now. In a few moments she'd know whether she understood the questions . . . or if she'd have to cheat.

Cheat. It was a word Tilly hated. She believed in

being honest and working hard. That was something positive her parents *had* done for her – they'd given her a really strong sense of right and wrong. And they'd always taught her the value of hard work. What would they say if they could see her now? And what would Bobby think? Tilly felt horrible as she thought of her kind-hearted, hard-working brother, who'd never failed an exam in his life. He'd be so ashamed of her. They all would.

'OK, guys, you can turn your papers over,' Mr Brown said, returning to his desk. 'You have forty minutes to complete the test. Good luck!'

As Tilly turned her paper her hand trembled. Instantly, she knew she was in trouble. The page was filled with so many words. Some of the questions were practically whole paragraphs. She took a deep breath and stared hard at the first question. It didn't have as many words as the others so maybe she'd be able to figure it out.

Jhon ahs 27 appels and Jnae has 3. What

epcretnage of the paples do ecah of tehm
have?

She focused on the numbers: 27 and 3. Was the question asking her to add them up? She could do that. 27 plus 3 made 30. But it seemed way too easy. There had to be more to it than that. What did 'epcretnage' mean? She slipped her hand into her pocket and slid the card up her sleeve. Behind her, someone coughed loudly, causing her to jump. Had they seen what she was doing? She took another deep breath. They couldn't possibly have seen. Nobody could. Her hand was still in her pocket. But if she took the card out . . .? Her heart started racing and a cold sweat erupted on her skin. She looked back at the question but she was so stressed now that the letters were dancing all over the place. The tightness in her throat grew until she felt as if she couldn't breathe. If her mum took her out of WEDA she didn't know how she'd cope. She'd be put in a school where most of the day would be spent in academic lessons, being tortured like this. She'd no longer have the freedom of daily dance classes or Il Bello or rehearsals for shows. Her life would be *over*. But . . .

If she got caught cheating she'd lose her place at WEDA too. And even worse, she'd be thrown out in shame. She was doomed. She'd never be able to face Il Bello again. At the thought of not seeing Andre and the rest of the crew again, the tears that had been threatening to break like a storm all week finally burst and started rolling down her face. Tilly was mortified. She was crying – in the middle of an exam, in front of all of her classmates – like a baby. She tried to be strong, to stop the tears from coming, but now they'd started they just wouldn't stop. She had to get out of there. She couldn't let anyone see. She heard her chair clattering to the ground as she stumbled to her feet. But the sound felt muffled, like she was underwater, drowning in tears.

'Tilly. What's wrong?' Mr Brown's voice was muffled too.

Tilly stumbled past him and out of the door. She ran down the corridor, not knowing where she was going, just running and running until she found a way outside. She burst through a fire exit and raced towards the back of the building, tripping and stumbling on the icy ground. Finally, she made it to the stable. She let herself in and sank to the floor, crying loud, hard sobs.

She'd only been there a couple of minutes when the door crashed open and Billie burst in.

'I knew you'd come here,' she gasped, leaning on the wall to catch her breath.

'Wait – but . . .' Tilly wiped her eyes. 'Why aren't you doing your test?'

Billie looked at her like she was crazy. 'Because I was worried about you.'

'Won't you get into trouble?'

Billie shook her head. 'Mr Brown said I could go and look for you. Even if he hadn't, I would have come.' She crouched on the floor in front of Tilly and took hold of her hands. 'What's wrong,

Tillz? I hate seeing you like this.'

'I don't want to talk about it.' Tilly pulled her hands away and wiped her eyes.

'But it might help. There might be something I can do to make you feel better.'

'No it won't . . . and no you can't.' The thought of telling Billie that she'd almost cheated in the Maths test made Tilly's skin crawl.

'But I'm your best friend.' Billie looked at her sadly. 'Aren't I?'

Tilly glanced away. 'I just don't like talking about feelings and stuff.'

Billie sighed. 'OK. You don't like talking, so why don't we dance?' She got to her feet and took her iPhone from her pocket. 'This is my dance to you,' she said, plugging the phone into the studio stereo. 'You're welcome to join in.'

A slow, soulful song started playing. As Tilly listened to the opening lines she felt fresh tears forming in her eyes. The song was all about soul sisters and the unbreakable bond between girlfriends. Billie started dancing in a beautiful blend of ballet and street, freestyling her way over to Tilly and holding out her hands. Tilly got to her feet.

'Just dance how you're feeling,' Billie whispered.

Tilly closed her eyes. She thought about how much Billie meant to her and her heart felt as if it might burst. She began moving around Billie, mirroring her dance of friendship and love. And, as she moved, all the thoughts and fears of the past few days came bubbling up from where she'd kept them, so tightly trapped inside. Even though the music was slow she started spinning faster and faster, spinning all the stressful thoughts from her body. She pictured them splattering against the walls and sliding into a puddle on the floor. And then some fresh new thoughts started forming in her mind. She wasn't a cheater. She was a dancer. Her dyslexia might make her feel small but dancing – dancing made her shine. Just like a crazy, beat-up diamond. Billie was her best friend. She'd just said so. She wasn't bored of Tilly. Or disappointed with her. She didn't think Tilly was dumb. She really cared about her. Tilly stopped spinning and looked at her friend. She was grooving slowly to the melody, her arms flung open as wide as her heart.

'I'm so sorry,' Tilly said, her eyes filling with yet more tears.

'What for?' Billie danced over as the song came to an end.

'For being such a rubbish friend.'

'You're not a rubbish friend. Shall we sit down?' Billie gestured to the cluster of brightly coloured beanbags in the corner.

Tilly nodded and followed her over.

'You do still want to be my friend, then?' Billie asked.

'Of course!' Tilly laughed. 'It's funny cos I was going to ask you the exact same thing.'

'But why?' Billie looked so confused at the idea that she might not be Tilly's friend it made Tilly's heart sing. 'Look, I don't know what's been going on with you and I understand if you don't want to talk about it but I just want you to know that I'm your best friend forever, OK? I'll never judge you and I'm always here for you, no matter what.'

'Oh, Bill.' Tilly looked down at her lap. 'I'm so sorry. OK, I'll tell you. At Christmas my mum said she'd take me out of WEDA if I didn't get my grades up. But it's so hard. My dyslexia – it's like my mind is a prison and no words can get in or out. And I can't ask the teachers for extra time or help because then Cassandra will find out and she'll make my life hell and then I'll probably end up pushing her off a mountain or something and –'

'What?' Billie stared at her. 'Why would you push her off a mountain?'

'Long story. The point is, I've been so stressed about it. And I found out at the weekend that my mum called Miss Murphy and asked her to email her all my grades. That's why I freaked out in the Maths test. I couldn't work out what the questions said.'

Billie moved closer and took hold of her hand.

This time Tilly didn't pull hers away. It was weird. For so long she'd thought that talking about your problems only made them worse but sharing them with Billie like this felt kind of good. Tilly took a deep breath.

'I – uh – I was even thinking about cheating.'

'Cheating? How?'

Tilly took the card from her pocket and handed it to Billie. She felt a sudden rush of shame. Would Billie *still* want to be friends with her? 'I didn't, though. Honestly. I didn't look at it once.'

There was a silence, which probably only lasted a couple of seconds but to Tilly felt like hours.

'But how is this cheating?' Billie asked. 'This doesn't give any of the answers, it's just some words and symbols.'

'To help me with the questions.' Tilly bowed her head in embarrassment. 'Sometimes I can't understand what they're asking.'

'Yes, because you're dyslexic,' Billie said. 'Cheating is when you look at the answers in a test or if you'd brought in explanations of how to do things. This wouldn't have been cheating at all. If the teachers knew how hard it was for you I'm sure they'd let you use something like this in a test. You just need to tell them. Who cares what Cassandra thinks? You can't let your fear of her make you lose your place at WEDA.'

'I'm not afraid of her!' Tilly exclaimed. 'I'm afraid of what I'll do to her if she keeps on taunting me for being stupid.'

'What, like pushing her off a mountain?'

'Exactly!' Tilly gave Billie a weak smile. 'So, you don't think I'm a cheater then? You still want to be my friend?'

Billie grinned at her. 'Of course!'

'And you're not disappointed in me?'

'No! You're my *she*-ro.'

Tilly did a double-take. 'What? Why?'

'Because it must be so hard to have dyslexia, but you don't let it stop you from chasing your dreams.' Billie looked up at Tilly's flamingo mural. 'Look at your artwork. And your dancing. You're so talented. And actually, you're amazing with words, too.'

Tilly laughed. 'No way.'

'You are. That thing you read out in class last week was incredible.'

'But I didn't read it. I just made it up on the spot.'

'Exactly! I could never make something up on the spot like that.'

'Really?' Tilly stared at her, unsure if she was lying just to make her feel good, but Billie looked deadly serious.

'You're super intelligent, Tilly. Don't let your dyslexia or that stupid Ice Queen Cassandra make you think that you're not.'

Tilly felt a massive weight lifting. 'Thank you,' she murmured.

Billie put her arm round her shoulder and pulled her close. 'You're not going to lose your place at WEDA,' she said firmly. 'There's no way I or the rest of the crew are going to allow it.'

CHAPTER
ELEVEN

Tilly stood outside Miss Murphy's office and took a deep breath. Her heart was pounding as if she was about to go on stage. But this was much less fun – she was about to explain to WEDA's Head of Dance and Wellness why she'd run out of a test. Billie had persuaded Tilly to go and see Mr Brown after the test had finished. He'd been really nice about it, but told Tilly that she had to go and see Miss Murphy to explain what had happened. Tilly took a deep breath and knocked on the door.

'Come in,' Miss Murphy called.

Tilly opened the door and stepped inside the office. Miss Murphy was sitting behind a large wooden desk, backlit by the window behind her. She took off her glasses and placed them beside her laptop.

'Hello, Tilly.'

'Hello, Miss. Mr Brown said I should come and see you.'

Miss Murphy nodded. 'That's right. He told me that you ran out of your Maths test. He was very worried about you.'

'I'm sorry.' Tilly looked down, staring at the swirls on the plush carpet until it made her eyes hurt.

'Would you like to tell me what happened?'

Tilly squirmed. This was one of those questions adults asked that wasn't really a question at all. She could hardly say no. But the thought of telling Miss Murphy how she was feeling made her cringe.

'Why don't you take a seat?' Miss Murphy pointed to one of the chairs in front of her desk.

Tilly nodded gratefully and sat down.

'Andre speaks very highly of you, you know.' Miss Murphy leaned back in her huge leather chair and smiled. 'He's shown me the blog you do together, and your artwork. It's very good.'

'Thank you.' Tilly gulped.

'So, why did you run out of your test this morning?' Miss Murphy asked gently.

Tilly thought about making something up; pretending that she'd been feeling sick, but then she remembered how much better she'd felt when she told Billie the truth. She realized it was a big gamble; that if she told Miss Murphy that her dyslexia was a much bigger problem than she'd been making out, Miss Murphy would probably tell her mum, but Tilly was so tired of pretending that everything was OK when it wasn't.

'I – uh – I was having trouble reading some of the questions,' she said, stumbling over the words.

'Having trouble reading them? Do you think you need an eye test?'

'No. It's not my eyes – it's – it's my dyslexia.'

'Your dyslexia?' Miss Murphy put her glasses back on and tapped something into her computer. 'But your teachers should be aware of your dyslexia. It's right here on your school record that you were diagnosed a couple of years ago. You should be being given extra support.'

'I don't want extra support. I – uh – I told my teachers I didn't need it.' Tilly's face began to burn.

'But why?' Miss Murphy stared at her.

'I was embarrassed. I didn't want to look stupid. But . . .'

Miss Murphy nodded, encouraging her to go on. 'But?'

'It's been so hard pretending everything's OK when it isn't. And my mum got really mad when she saw my end-of-term results. She thinks I use my dyslexia as an excuse for not working hard enough. She thinks all I care about is dance, which is kind of true, but there's no way I want to leave WEDA . . . so I've been really panicking.'

'Who said anything about you leaving WEDA?'

'My mum.' Tilly looked down at her lap glumly. 'She said if I don't get my grades up she'll remove me from WEDA – make me go to a normal school.'

'I see.' Miss Murphy nodded again, looking

thoughtful for a moment. 'Well, we can't let that happen.'

Tilly looked at her in surprise. 'Really?'

Miss Murphy nodded. 'You're an exceptional student, Tilly, a real asset to the academy. Your dyslexia isn't an excuse, it's something you need proper support with. And needing support does not mean that you're stupid and it's nothing to be embarrassed about.'

Tilly felt tears of gratitude welling in her eyes. 'Seriously?'

'Of course. And you leave your mum to me. She had been in touch, asking how you were getting on. I'll tell her that we've identified an issue with your dyslexia and that we're going to do everything in our power to get your academic grades up.'

'Thank you!'

'And I hope you realize that you could see this as a positive,' Miss Murphy continued.

'Oh, I do. Thank you so much for being so supportive.'

Miss Murphy shook her head. 'I didn't mean that. I meant, having dyslexia.'

Tilly stared at her. 'How is that a positive?'

Miss Murphy smiled at her. 'Because it's like having a superpower.'

'A superpower?'

She nodded. 'Being dyslexic might mean that you struggle with the spellings of words but it also means that other parts of your brain are over-developed as a result.'

Tilly struggled to understand what Miss Murphy was saying. She was so used to feeling dumb it felt crazy thinking of her dyslexia as a superpower. 'Like what?'

'Well, people with dyslexia tend to be highly creative so I'd say that your talent as an artist is in large part down to your dyslexia. And lots of people with the condition are also way better at seeing the bigger picture of things – you don't get lost in the smaller details.' Miss Murphy tapped something into her computer. 'Here we go,' she said, looking at the screen. 'Here's a list of all the mega-successful people who have dyslexia. I'm going to print it out for you. Even Albert Einstein is on the list.'

'Albert Einstein? Wasn't he, like, one of the brainiest people who ever lived?'

Miss Murphy nodded. 'I told you, it's a superpower.'

Tilly felt giddy from relief. This meeting could not have gone better.

Miss Murphy printed out the list and handed it to her. 'I'm going to get a plan in place to support you in your lessons. You're not on your own with this any more, Tilly, OK?'

Tilly nodded. She only hoped her mum would be as supportive.

For the rest of the day, Tilly felt as if she was floating on a cloud of happiness. Even the prospect of a tap rehearsal with Cassandra last period didn't faze her. She had a superpower – Miss Murphy had said so – something that made her different from Cassandra and all the others. Different, but not worse. Tilly didn't even bother applying her usual extra layer of make-up. She marched into the studio and over to the barre.

'I hear you ran out of your Maths test,' Cassandra said, smiling at her sweetly. 'What was wrong? Couldn't you answer any of the questions?'

Tilly held her head up high and smiled back at her. 'No, I'd heard there was someone in reception selling new personalities. I thought I'd go and get you one.' She turned away, grinning.

'You stupid –' Cassandra began, just as Mrs Jones walked into the room.

'Cassandra!' Mrs Jones barked.

Tilly's grin widened. Today just kept on getting better. And this time, when they danced, she didn't let Cassandra's steps throw her off. Instead she finally managed to switch off her negative thoughts and enjoy the dance, poking fun at herself and being silly. Dancing to the 'Duelling Banjos' was actually a lot of fun!

At the end of the rehearsal, Mrs Jones nodded her head and smiled. 'Thank you, girls. I think it's finally starting to come together. Very good effort today, Tilly – you've really begun to make the dance your own.'

Tilly grinned. 'Thanks, Mrs Jones.'

Cassandra's smile looked so forced Tilly was surprised her jaw didn't crack.

As Tilly headed to the stable after school, she saw Andre and Billie walking towards her.

'Where are you two going?' she asked.

'Where are *we three* going?' Andre replied as he and Billie linked each of Tilly's arms and turned her back to face the way she came.

'But I thought we were rehearsing with the crew tonight?'

Andre shook his head. 'Something more important came up.'

'What's more important than Il Bello?'

'*You* are,' he replied. 'I heard what happened in your Maths test. And Billie told me about your chat.'

'He made me tell him,' Billie said sheepishly. 'He was really worried about you.'

'Why didn't you tell me what was up?' Andre said.

'I'm sorry.' Tilly smiled. It was weird. For so long she'd dreaded Andre finding out about her academic struggles but now he knew, she felt nothing but relief.

'That's all right. Just don't let it happen again, OK?'

'I won't. Anyway, it's all good now. I went to see your mum and she was amazing.'

Andre grinned proudly. 'Yeah, she's not so bad.'

'So, where are we going?' Tilly asked.

'We're taking you out,' Billie said.

'Where to?'

'Can't tell you, it's a surprise,' Andre said. 'But what I can tell you is you need to get changed asap. Sweaty dance gear is not going to cut it where we're going.'

After Tilly had changed, Andre and Billie took her to the station and they got on a train to London.

All the way up there Tilly begged to know where they were going but Andre and Billie refused to crack. They ended up taking the Tube to Southbank. Tilly gasped as they emerged from the Underground and she saw the London skyline all lit up.

'Are we going on the London Eye?' she asked.

Andre shook his head. He and Billie led her into a building close to the London Eye called the Royal Festival Hall. They took the lift up to the fourth floor . . . and emerged into a library.

Tilly's heart sank. 'You've brought me to a library?'

'Yes, but not just any old library,' Andre replied.

'It's a poetry library,' Billie explained.

'*Great.*' Tilly was barely able to hide her disappointment. Why would they bring her to a place full of books when they knew how hard it was for her to read? A space had been cleared in the middle of the library and was filled with rows of chairs. The chairs were full of people laughing and chattering, and there was a microphone set up at the front.

'There's a poetry show on here tonight,' Billie explained.

'But it's not just any old poetry show,' Andre said.

'It's spoken-word poetry,' Billie said with a grin.

Tilly shrugged. 'What's spoken-word poetry?'

'Wait and see,' Andre replied. 'I think you're gonna love it.'

Tilly sat down, but she wasn't so sure. She really appreciated that they were trying to do something nice for her but did it really have to be something to do with words and writing? She'd much rather have stayed at WEDA rehearsing with Il Bello.

A man with small round glasses and a goatee beard went up to the mic. 'Hey, everyone, welcome to Spoken Word Heard. We have some amazing spoken-word performers here tonight so you're in for a real treat.'

'Please tell me what spoken word is,' Tilly whispered to Andre.

'Just wait and see,' he replied mysteriously.

'First up,' the host said, 'we have Natty Dread. Please give him a warm welcome.'

Everyone started clapping as a young guy with short dreadlocks went up to the mic. Tilly noticed that he wasn't holding anything. How was he going to read poetry without a book?

The guy took the mic from the stand. Then he began speaking and it was like all time stood still. What was coming from his mouth was like no poetry Tilly had ever heard. His words ebbed and flowed like a tide. They were strung together in a hypnotic rhythm and, even though there was no music playing, there was a melody to them that made Tilly want to dance. She could tell that Andre and Billie were feeling the same way too. Out of the corner of her eye she could see their heads nodding and their bodies swaying in time with the beat. As the poem came to an end Tilly looked at them.

'Oh my God, that was amazing!'

'Yep,' Andre replied, his eyes wide.

Tilly didn't say another word until the end of the

show. She wasn't able to. The performers had her mesmerized. She loved the fact that all their poems were about things that really mattered – like racism and bullying and poverty. And they were spoken in a way she could really relate to. There were no stuck-up, posh words but real words, with real feeling.

It was only once they were back outside that any of them were able to speak.

'So, what did you think?' Billie asked her as they walked along the River Thames.

'It was so, so awesome.'

'Yes!' Andre exclaimed. 'We were really hoping you'd say that.'

'Why?'

Billie smiled as she linked Tilly's arm. 'Because we think you'd be an excellent spoken-word poet.'

'No way!'

'Why not?' Andre demanded.

'I hate writing!'

'But with spoken word you don't need to write,' Andre said.

'How would I remember anything?'

'You could record it – on your phone,' Billie said. 'Seriously. What you came up with in English the other day was just as good as anything we heard tonight.'

Tilly frowned. 'Really?'

Billie nodded.

'And all the stuff you tell me to write on Spotted is so good,' Andre said.

'We don't want you to hate words,' Billie said. 'Because we love the way you use them.'

Tilly looked out across the river, at the Houses of Parliament all lit up like a palace from a fairy-tale. And this day, which had started so horribly, was getting the most fairy-tale of endings.

'Promise you'll think about it?' Billie asked.

Tilly nodded. 'OK, I'll think about it.' On this magical night, anything felt possible.

CHAPTER
TWELVE

The next morning Tilly was woken by the sound of Naomi 'drat'-ing and moaning as she made her way to the bathroom. Tilly snuggled further beneath her duvet and smiled as memories from the day before drifted back to her: Miss Murphy telling her she was an asset to WEDA and that her dyslexia was a superpower. Dancing well in her tap rehearsal. Mrs Jones praising her in front of Cassandra. And then the spoken-word event with Andre and Billie.

As she thought of how the poets had made their words sing, her skin began to tingle, just like her and Andre's tingle test. Were her friends right? Could she create a spoken-word poem too? But what would she make it about? She thought about the poems she'd heard the night before. They'd all been about things the poets had been through. Challenges they'd faced and overcome. Just like the piece about her Christmas holiday. She thought back to that day, wracking her brains, trying to remember what she'd said. There'd been something about scrolling though social media; that had been good. She took her phone from her bedside cabinet and switched it to the recorder. 'Like a vacant scroll through social media,' she said quietly into it. Next door, she heard the toilet flush and she pressed pause. But then she heard Naomi turn on the bathroom tap so she started to record again. 'Like a vacant scroll through social media, waiting for a like.' What else had she said in class that day? Something about an emoji. 'Finding safety in an emoji.'

'Finding what?' Naomi said, returning from the bathroom.

'Nothing.' Tilly quickly turned the recorder off.

'Were you just talking in your sleep?' Naomi went over to her wardrobe and pulled out a

T-shirt and some sweatpants.

'Must have been,' Tilly replied, faking a yawn.

'I'm going for a run. Do you fancy it?' Naomi said as she dressed.

'No. I think I'll grab a few minutes' more sleep.'

Tilly waited until Naomi had gone, then she opened her laptop and put on a random music video. As the track started playing she got out of bed and allowed her body to slowly move to the tune.

'Like a vacant scroll through the timelines of social media, waiting for a like,' she murmured. 'Finding safety in an emoji, wishing . . . wishing life were as simple as the smile I portray to a world that's never paying attention.' It was weird, now she was moving her body the words came a lot easier. She closed her eyes and continued dancing, thinking of all the times she'd felt stupid and small recently. *When will it be my time to shine?* she thought. She grabbed her phone and recorded the line. 'When will it be my time to shine?' Then she carried on freestyling around the room, this time thinking of the release she felt whenever she did her artwork. 'The paint – no – the *spray* of my paint releases me from this prison that I'm in,' Tilly recorded on her phone. 'The spray of my paint releases me from this prison that I'm in. This impossibility to fit in.' Tilly smiled. There was something so satisfying about the rhythm of the words. 'My positivity . . . my positivity . . . never stands out *positively*.' Tilly was really enjoying this now. This combination of words and music and dance. But then her flow was interrupted by a loud knock on the door.

'Tilly!' Andre called from the corridor outside. 'Open this door immediately. I have an urgent LCO to talk to you about.'

'What on earth's an LCO?' Tilly asked, opening the door.

'Life. Changing. Opportunity,' Andre said.

'Life changing for who?' Tilly asked, sitting down on her bed.

'You.' Andre sat down next to her. 'I just saw an ad for an audition on DANCE NOW that would be perfect for you. Listen.' He pulled his phone from his pocket and started to read.

'*Are you a dancer with a really original look?*' Andre looked at Tilly. 'Er, yes.' He looked back at the phone. '*Do you enjoy experimenting with different dance styles?* Er, hello! *Would you describe yourself as willing to go the extra mile?* Abso-frickin-lutely! *Chart-topping band seek dancer for new video. Send headshot and CV to apply to audition.*' Andre put his phone down. 'This job has got your name written all over it.'

'Really?'

'Of course. And if you got it, it could be life changing.'

'How?'

Andre sat cross-legged, back ruler straight. 'Your mum thinks that dancing doesn't matter, right?'

Tilly sighed. 'Don't remind me.'

'She thinks that you need to do well academically or you'll never survive out there in the big, bad world.'

'Pretty much.'

'Well, this is your chance to prove her wrong. If you landed this job you could show her how you'd be able to make a living from your dancing.'

'Hmm.'

'And seriously, think how awesome it would be to be in a music video.' He nodded to Tilly's laptop, where another video had started playing. 'Major life goal.'

'Are you sure *you* don't want to go for it?' Tilly asked.

Andre shook his head. 'No. If it means helping you stay at WEDA I'm willing to make the US.'

'US?'

'Ultimate Sacrifice.'

Tilly laughed.

'I mean it, Tillz. We have to do everything we can to make your mum see sense.'

Tilly nodded. Then she looked back at her laptop. Dancing in a music video would be a major life goal achieved. The chances of her getting the job would be tiny but what did she really have to lose?

She looked at Andre and smiled. 'OK. I'll do it.'

*

Tilly's first lesson that morning was ballet. As she was warming up doing plies at the barre, allowing the stretch to take over her breath and her body, some more random lines started popping into her head. Of course, this time she wasn't able to break off from class to record them, so she had to keep repeating the lines over and over in her head so she didn't forget. As soon as the bell rang for break Tilly raced to the toilets, locked herself in a cubicle and recorded the words on her phone.

The same thing happened during her tap rehearsal with Cassandra. As she loosened her feet and allowed them to fly across the floor to the rhythm of the duelling banjos, more words popped into her head. Even when Cassandra tried to steal her thunder in front of Mrs Jones, Tilly didn't rise to the bait. She was too lost in the words and the beat.

At lunchtime she raced to the stable, eager to see Andre and Billie and update them. When she got to the studio Andre was already there, staring up at her flamingo mural, a thoughtful expression upon his face.

'What's up?' Tilly said.

'Nothing!' Andre said, spinning round, looking slightly guilty. 'How's your morning been?'

'Really good.' Tilly took her jacket off and started doing some stretches. 'You're going to be pleased with me.'

'Why?' Andre said, coming over to join her.

'I applied for that audition at break.'

'What audition?' Billie said, coming into the stable with MJ and Raf.

'It's for a music video,' Tilly replied. 'I probably haven't got a chance of getting it but –'

'Whoa!' Andre cried. 'Stop right there with the NST.'

'Andre!' Tilly sighed. 'Could *you* please stop right there with all the talking in initials. It's so confusing!'

'Yes,' Billie agreed. 'What does NST even mean?'

'Negative self-talk,' Andre said with a huff. 'OMG, you guys are so HTP!'

The others all started to groan.

'Hard to please!' Andre cried. 'OK, can we get back to the topic in question? AKA – sorry! Also known as . . .' he quickly corrected himself. '. . . Tilly's audition. And more importantly, all the "I probably haven't got a chance of getting it" baloney.' He gestured at the others to gather round. 'Now, I know you've had a lousy week, Tillz, but you seem to have forgotten one very important fact.'

Tilly looked at him blankly.

'You belong to the Il Bello street crew!' Andre exclaimed. 'We're your dance famalam. We've got your back, always. And we're going to do everything we can to make sure you ace this audition and convince your mum once and for all that dance is important and that you can stay at WEDA. Isn't that right?' He looked at the others and they all nodded in agreement.

'We'd do anything for you, sister,' Raf said, patting Tilly on the shoulder.

'Yes,' MJ said gruffly.

'And you know I'm always here for you,' Billie said, hugging her. 'Best friends forever, right?' she whispered in Tilly's ear.

'Guys, stop it! You're going to make me cry or something,' Tilly exclaimed.

'The time for crying is over,' Andre announced dramatically. 'It's more over than Ugg boots and tiger onesies.' He gave Billie a pointed stare.

'I love my tiger onesie,' she retorted.

Andre pursed his lips. 'We need to get our thinking caps on and figure out a way Tilly can slay this audition. They're looking for something really different – really unique. So why don't we see what we can come up with?'

As they all sat down around her, Tilly felt a warm glow inside. Andre was right. Il Bello was her family. And there was no way she was going to lose it without a fight.

'We need to think outside the box,' Andre said. 'Not just for the dance but for the look and the music too.'

'I have an idea,' Billie said.

They all looked at her expectantly.

'What if you danced to a spoken-word poem? That would be different and it would be so powerful.'

Tilly nodded slowly.

'Great idea!' Andre said. 'We just need to find a poem.'

'I – uh – I might be able to help with that,' Tilly said, feeling slightly embarrassed.

'What? How?' Billie stared at her. 'Oh my God, have you started writing one?'

Tilly nodded shyly. 'I don't know if it'll be any good but I'm willing to give it a try.'

'Awesome.' Andre grinned. 'OK, anyone got any ideas for her dance?'

'Why don't you try fusing some capoeira with your usual street style?' Raf suggested. 'I could teach you a couple of killer moves.'

'Yes!' Billie exclaimed. 'You could create a fusion of capoeira and voguing in a contemporary masterpiece!'

Tilly nodded again.

'Is there any way we could get her artwork into the audition too?' MJ asked.

'I don't think so,' Tilly said. 'I can hardly take the stable walls to the audition.'

'But we could film them,' Andre said excitedly. 'And use it as a background projection.'

Tilly pictured dancing in front of the image of the flamingo and her heart sang. All the random ideas from the crew were coming together to create something really special, something unique. She pictured herself in a crazy and wonderful outfit, topped off with the captain's hat with the flamingo motif. The whole audition would be a celebration of her overcoming her insecurities – from the poem to the background projections to her outfit and of course, her dance. As she hugged her knees into her chest one of the lines she'd recorded earlier came back to echo in her mind. Could this audition finally be her time to shine?

CHAPTER THIRTEEN

The following week, Tilly re-sat her Maths test. She was given extra time to complete it, which helped her figure out more of the words in the questions. All of her other teachers had been really supportive too, especially Mrs Jarvis, who even apologized to Tilly for being so hard on her. Dance rehearsals were going well – with the Investor Showcase looming, she and Cassandra had finally managed to put their differences aside and focus on bringing their all to the routine. Tilly had also got an audition for the music video and Il Bello were pulling out all the stops to help her slay it. The only cloud still on Tilly's horizon was her mum. Although Miss Murphy had called her about Tilly's dyslexia and tried to reassure her that her grades would now improve, she didn't seem convinced.

'We need to have a serious talk about this,' she'd said to Tilly in a tense phone call after. 'If your dyslexia is as bad as Miss Murphy says then we need to think about whether WEDA is the best place for you.'

Whether WEDA is the best place for you . . . Her mum's words came echoing back to Tilly now, as she tried to put the finishing touches to her spoken-word piece with Billie.

'Are you OK?' Billie asked, switching off the camera on her phone. They'd come to the stable so she could film Tilly performing her poem. 'Did you forget the words?'

'Yes . . . no.' Tilly frowned. 'Sorry, I'm just worrying about what my mum said.'

Billie came over and gave her a hug. 'Don't. It's going to be fine. When she sees that your grades have improved she'll have no reason to take you out of here.'

Tilly sighed. 'But what if they don't improve?'

'They will. The teachers are all giving you extra support now. They're bound to get better.'

Tilly nodded but she couldn't help feeling worried. There was only so much the teachers could do for her. The fact was, she still found it really hard to read and write, and no amount of extra time for assignments or in tests was going to change that. She took a deep breath. She had to stay focused. With the music video audition and the Investor Showcase just around the corner, she couldn't afford to let fear get the better of her.

'I've got an idea,' Billie said. 'Why don't you try talking about how you're feeling right now – about your mum. It might help you to get it off your chest. And maybe we can weave it into the poem.'

'OK.' Tilly closed her eyes and took a few deep breaths. How *was* she feeling right now? How was her mum making her feel? Unnoticed, small, unable to shine. She opened her mouth and let the words flow. 'The true me goes unnoticed, shrunk – no – *dwarfed* by letters, blocking my unique intelligence. When will it be my time to shine?' Then she thought of how afraid she was of her mum removing her from WEDA. 'When fear takes my tongue I quiver and shrink . . . back into my box of difference.'

'This is great,' Billie said softly. 'Just keep going. Say what you need to say.'

Tilly felt a warm burst of confidence at her friend's praise. 'Be you, be fearless, be authentic, be weird, be real,' she said, her voice rising. 'Be the flight of the bumblebee spreading a beautiful crew's message to the masses.'

'Yes!' Billie cried.

'This false system tortures a dyslexic mind to strive for its impossible perfection.' Tilly opened her eyes, shocked at where the stream of words had come from.

Billie was grinning from ear to ear. 'Oh, Tilly, this is so good!'

'What's so good?' Andre burst into the stable,

holding an armful of clothes. He was followed swiftly by Raf and MJ.

'Tilly's poem,' Billie replied. 'It's going to be awesome.'

'When can we hear it?' Raf asked.

'When it's finished,' Billie replied firmly. She turned to Tilly. 'I'll send you what we recorded today, so you can play it back and memorize it.'

'Thank you.' Tilly watched as Andre came over and dumped the clothes on one of the beanbags.

'Your Fearless Fashion audition wardrobe has arrived,' he announced. 'And it's all vegan, so you can wear it with a clear conscience.'

'You want me to wear all of that?' Tilly stared at the huge pile of clothes.

'No! But I wasn't exactly sure of the look we should go for, so I brought fifteen different options. We should feature your fearless flamingo hat as well!'

'Fifteen!' Billie exclaimed.

Andre frowned. 'Do you think I should have

brought more? I was going to but I didn't want to overdo it.'

Tilly and Billie burst out laughing.

'No. Fifteen is plenty, Dre,' Tilly replied.

'Why don't you and Tilly go up to the dorm rooms to work on the look?' Raf asked. 'While we – you know – get the background projection finished?' There was something about the way he asked the question, and the way Billie gave him a knowing grin, that made Tilly instantly suspicious.

'Oh yes,' Andre said with an equally knowing nod. He picked up the clothes with one arm and took hold of Tilly with the other.

'What's going on?' Tilly asked.

'Nothing!' Bille, Raf, MJ and Andre all chorused in unison, leaving Tilly totally convinced that something was up.

'Come on!' Andre said, whisking her out the door.

Back in Tilly's dorm room, after much deliberation, they decided on a military-style jacket with a diamante trim, a lavender vest top and green and purple trousers with a peacock print.

'Because peacocking is all about revealing your true authentic self,' Tilly said, admiring the trousers in the mirror. 'I'm going to have to change my hair colour, though.'

'Yeah, I reckon you should go for lavender,' Andre said, standing behind her and looking at her reflection.

Tilly nodded. Although she felt really nervous at the prospect of the audition, seeing her outfit come together definitely made her feel more confident. She quickly got changed back into her sweatpants and T-shirt. 'Shall we go back to the stable, see how the others are doing?'

'Yeah, sure, but – er – just let me just check something first.' Andre dialled a number on his phone. 'Hey, Billie, is everything, you know, OK?'

Tilly watched him curiously. Why was he acting so weird?

Andre nodded. 'OK, great. We're on our way.'

When Tilly and Andre got back to the stable he

turned to her and grinned. 'Are you ready?' he said.

'What for?'

Andre opened the door. The other members of the crew were all gathered around Tilly's flamingo mural.

'We hope you don't mind, but we added a little something to your artwork before we filmed it for your audition,' Andre said, leading her over.

The others turned to face her. They all looked really nervous. Tilly gazed up at the flamingo. The crew had spray-painted some words inside the huge bubble-gum bubble. She stared up at them, trying to make out what they said.

'They're the words we think of when we think of you,' Billie explained. 'Shall we each read the word we chose?' The others nodded and one by one they read out a word.

'Fierce,' Raf said, putting his arm round Tilly.

'Authentic,' MJ said, avoiding eye contact with Tilly but with a smile on his lips.

'Beautiful and Swag!' Andre said loudly with

a grin. 'I couldn't choose just one.'

'Independent,' Billie said, taking hold of Tilly's hand.

Tilly felt really choked. 'Guys! This is amazing!'

'So you don't mind us messing with your picture?' MJ asked, looking concerned.

'Of course not. It's such a cool thing to do. Thank you.'

The rest of Il Bello all crowded round her for a group hug.

'You're gonna slay this audition,' Andre said.

Tilly nodded but the warmth she felt from their kindness and support was laced with an icy fear. What if she didn't slay it? What if she failed? How would she convince her mum that she could make a success of dance? How would she persuade her to let her stay at WEDA?

CHAPTER
FOURTEEN

The day of the audition dawned bright and crisp. As Tilly sat up in bed and looked at the sunlight streaming in through the curtains she hoped it was a good omen. Luckily, the audition fell late on a Friday afternoon when there were no lessons, so all of Il Bello would be able to come with her for moral support. But first she had the morning's classes to get through.

The first lesson of the day was Maths.

'Ah, Tilly,' Mr Brown said, as she walked into the classroom. 'I've marked your exam paper.'

Tilly went over to his desk, her heart thumping. *Please, please, please let it be a good grade. Or a better grade at least,* she silently pleaded.

Mr Brown took the paper from a folder on his desk. There was a big red D at the top of the page. It had a plus sign next to it, but it was still a D. Tilly's heart sank.

'This is a definite improvement on your end-of-term paper last year,' Mr Brown said. 'You were just a couple of marks away from getting a C.'

But this only made Tilly feel worse. If only she'd tried that little bit harder. If only she'd got those extra two marks. It didn't matter that she'd gone from a D minus to a D plus – as far as her mum was concerned she'd still be a D grade student. D for Dumb. And her mum would still have a reason for taking her out of WEDA.

'Well done, Tilly,' Mr Brown said, handing her the paper. 'If you carry on at this rate we'll have you up to a C grade by the end of term.'

But that was no consolation to Tilly. What if her mum wasn't prepared to wait until the end of term? What if she took her out of WEDA now? The lesson passed by in a blur as Tilly tried to think of things to say to her mum to try to excuse her Maths result. But it was no good. There was nothing she could say.

'Are you OK?' Billie whispered, halfway through the class.

Tilly nodded. But inside she felt a long, long way from OK. Anxiety fluttered in her ribcage and her stomach churned. This was the worst way to feel right before an audition. Especially an audition that now meant so much. Everything was rested on getting this job and proving to her mum that she could make a success of being a dancer.

'Remember the words,' Billie whispered.

'What words?' Tilly whispered back.

'Inside the bubble-gum bubble.'

Tilly closed her eyes and pictured the words Il Bello had added to her painting. The words that they thought of when they thought of her. FIERCE, AUTHENTIC, BEAUTIFUL, SWAG, INDEPENDENT. That was how her friends saw her. FIERCE, AUTHENTIC, BEAUTIFUL, SWAG,

INDEPENDENT. She took a deep breath, as if trying to inhale the words and their meaning, until gradually, they chased the anxiety away. She might not be an A-grade student but she was fierce and strong. She was authentic and real. She was full of swag and style. And she *was* independent. She could do this.

Tilly turned to Billie and smiled. 'Thank you,' she whispered.

The audition was taking place in a studio in London. As soon as the morning's classes finished, all of Il Bello headed for the station. Andre was carrying Tilly's 'wardrobe'. Raf had the film he and MJ had made of Tilly's artwork for the background projection. Billie had brought the recording of Tilly's poem and a lucky crystal that her uncle had brought back from a trip to Thailand. MJ had insisted on carrying Tilly's bag. Although it was only Tilly actually doing the audition it felt like a total team effort.

'Thanks so much, guys,' Tilly said as they took their seats on the London-bound train. 'I'd never have been able to do this without you.'

'Yes you would,' Andre replied. 'It just wouldn't have been nearly as fabulous.'

The others all fell about laughing and Tilly felt the last of her anxiety fade away. All the work was done now. She had to forget about test results and school and teachers and her mum and focus solely on her dance.

The studio was tucked away down a side street off Euston Road. As they stood waiting to cross the road, and a stream of buses, black cabs and cyclists all zoomed past, Tilly let the energy and noise of London soak into her. *You've got this!* she told herself. *You're going to slay it!* The soundtrack of car horns and police sirens and people yelling and chatting and laughing all helped build the buzz she was now feeling. *Buzzing like the flight of the bumblebee, spreading a beautiful crew's message to the masses.* The line from her poem played inside her head, spurring her on, making her feel invincible. By the time they got across the road, Tilly was so pumped she felt like throwing her head back and roaring. Who cared what her mum thought? Who cared about stupid dyslexia? D didn't stand for Dumb any more – it stood for Dance! And Tilly was going to dance all of the doubt and the dumbness and the disappointment away.

She felt a bit wobbly again when they got to the studio and she saw all the other dancers waiting – especially the ones with flawless skin. While the rest of Il Bello set up camp at the end of the corridor, she slipped into a disabled toilet and locked the door. She needed a bit of time on her own. Tilly looked at herself in the mirror. At her freshly dyed lavender hair and her peacock blue eyeliner. She took her fearless flamingo captain's hat from her bag and put it on. In the advert for the audition they'd asked for a dancer who was different, but was she *too* different? There certainly wasn't another dancer waiting outside who looked anything like her. But was that a bad thing or a good thing? She took a deep breath. It was a good thing, she decided. It had to be. Because who else could she be other than her true self? How could she ever shine if she hid behind convention? She looked herself straight in the eye. 'Be fearless, be authentic, be you,' she said firmly. Then she unlocked the door and went outside.

When Tilly's name was called for her audition, the rest of Il Bello gathered round, like they did before any crew performance.

'You're gonna be awesome,' Andre said.

'Good luck.' Billie kissed her on the cheek.

'You're going to do great,' MJ said.

Raf placed one of his strong arms round her shoulders. '*Buena suerte*,' he whispered in her ear.

'What does that mean?'

'Good luck, in Spanish.' His eyes twinkled as he grinned at her.

'Come on, let's go,' Andre said, taking Tilly's arm. Even though Raf and MJ had created the background projection for Tilly's audition, Andre had insisted on being the one to go in with her and set it up.

They walked down the long corridor and into the studio at the end. Two choreographers – a woman and a man – were sitting behind a table in the far corner.

'Hi, Tilly,' the woman said, looking at her CV. 'Do you have your music?'

'Yes. Well, it's not exactly music.' Tilly blushed as she took her phone over to them.

'What do you mean?' the guy asked.

'It's hard to explain. It's probably best to just play it and see,' Tilly said.

'Don't mind me,' Andre called as he set up the projector.

'Er, who is that?' the woman asked, raising her eyebrows.

'He's just setting up a –'

'I'm her manager,' Andre interrupted. 'I'm setting up the background projection. Would it be OK if I dimmed the studio lights?'

The choreographers exchanged looks, causing Tilly's heart to pound. What if they said no?

'OK,' the guy said eventually.

As Andre dimmed the lights Tilly took her spot in the centre of the floor. It was weird. Even though there was so much resting on this audition, she felt a sudden calmness. The moment had arrived and she was more than ready for it.

The light from the projector flickered into life. An image of Tilly's flamingo danced upon the wall. She took a breath and waited for her spoken-word track to begin.

'Like a vacant scroll through social media, waiting for a like,' her voice echoed around the studio. Tilly began dancing her interpretation of the words. 'Finding safety in an emoji, wishing that life were as simple as the smile I show to an online world.'

As the words of the poem became louder and more forceful, Tilly switched from the smooth flow of contemporary to voguing, cutting sharp shapes with her body in time to the rhythm of her words. Whenever she danced to music she found it easy to lose herself in the rhythm, but dancing to her own words and images took this to a whole new level. She wasn't just dancing her emotions, she was speaking them and seeing them too. Somewhere in the background, she heard the door open and close, the sound of footsteps making their way to the choreographers' table. But nothing could pull her focus now, she was completely lost in the dance. Finally, the poem came to an end.

'So, while I wait for you to notice?' Tilly did a back walk into a handspring. 'I'm taking my time to shine.' She pulled a perfect leg tilt, staying motionless throughout the pause in the poem. 'Cos my time to shine?' She melted to the ground into a backwards roll over her shoulder, her legs fanning over her head. Then she rolled up through her body until she was standing tall. 'Is now.'

Tilly opened her eyes and looked straight at the choreographers' table. She could see the silhouettes of three people sitting there but now the projection had ended it was too dark to make out who the third person was. Andre turned the studio lights back up. The third person was a guy with dark, cropped hair. He was wearing a grey T-shirt and there were three thick black rings tattooed around one of his arms. He was holding his phone up as if he'd been filming Tilly. Then he placed it on the table and began to clap. Tilly frowned. He looked really familiar. The tattoos looked really familiar. But she was still so buzzing from the audition she couldn't work out where she knew him from.

'That was dope!' the guy said. He had an American accent. The choreographers nodded in agreement.

Tilly's heart began to race as she finally realized where she'd seen those tattoos before. It was Tyler Joseph – the singer from Twenty One Pilots! 'Is – is this – is the audition for you?' she stammered.

Tyler Joseph laughed and nodded. 'Sure is.'

'Wow. It's – it's so nice to meet you.' *Keep your*

cool! Tilly could practically hear Andre screaming in her head. But how could she keep her cool? She'd just danced in front of one half of Twenty One Pilots. She'd just auditioned to be in one of their videos! And Tyler Joseph had said he thought her audition was dope! She glanced at Andre. His mouth was hanging open in amazement. He looked as shocked as she was.

'Great work,' Tyler said.

'Thank you, sir. I mean, Mr Joseph.' *What is wrong with you?!* Imaginary Andre yelled in her head. *Why are you calling him that?! He's not a flipping teacher!*

'That was an excellent audition, Tilly,' the woman choreographer said. 'We'll be in touch.'

'Thank you. Thank you so much.' Tilly started backing out of the room, not wanting to take her eyes off Tyler Joseph in case it was all just a dream.

As soon as she and Andre got out of the studio they looked at each other in disbelief.

'Oh my God, Tyler frickin' Joseph!' Andre

exclaimed. 'You just auditioned for Tyler frickin' Joseph!'

They raced down the corridor to where Il Bello were waiting.

'How did it go?' Billie asked, running over to meet them.

'You'll never guess what happened,' Tilly said, gasping. 'The video's for Twenty One Pilots. Their singer just watched me audition!'

'Oh my God.' Billie's eyes widened. 'That's amazing!'

'How did it go?' Raf asked.

'Did the background projection work?' MJ asked.

'Yes. It was awesome,' Andre said.

Billie grabbed hold of Tilly's arm. 'Do you think you've got the job? What did they say?'

'They said they'd be in touch.' Tilly frowned. The excitement she'd been feeling started being eaten away by doubt. 'But what does that mean? They might just have been being polite. What if they never call? What if they were messing with my mind?'

'I spy with my little eye something beginning with PASD,' Andre said.

'What's PASD?' Tilly asked.

'Post-audition Stress Disorder,' he replied. 'Come on, let's go get some emergency hot chocolate.'

CHAPTER
FIFTEEN

The following week it was the Investor Showcase. Tilly always woke with butterflies in her stomach on the day of a show, but this time it felt as if the usual butterflies had brought all of their families and friends along too. Not only did she have a major showcase to dance in but she'd also be seeing her mum and they'd be having The Conversation. She wasn't sure which she was more nervous about. Unable to stand the anxious thoughts crowding her mind, Tilly got up and got dressed. Then she switched on her phone and checked her emails. She'd been checking obsessively since the day of the audition but she still hadn't heard anything. She sighed. She obviously hadn't got the job. The one thing she'd been hoping to use to convince her mum to let her stay at WEDA hadn't happened. Now she had nothing.

After a quick breakfast, Tilly did some warm-up stretches, checking in with her body, easing her muscles into life. This was what she was born to do – live her dreams through her body, through her dance. She couldn't bear the thought of being made to go to a so-called normal school, stuck behind a desk for hours on end, stuck behind the bars of her dyslexia. The thought of what might be about to happen made her heart break.

Her phone started ringing and for a brief, bright moment, Tilly imagined it was the music video people offering her the job. But one look at the caller ID made her heart sink. It was her mum.

'Hello,' she said nervously.

'Hi, Tilly,' her mum said. 'We've just arrived.'

Tilly looked at the time. The showcase wasn't due to start for another two hours. They were so early. *Why* were they so early? Tilly's mouth went dry.

Was it because her mum wanted to see Miss Murphy to tell her Tilly would be leaving WEDA?

'Tilly? Are you there?' her mum said. In the background Tilly heard her dad making a joke about parking the car. Her mum didn't laugh.

'Yes – I – I'll come down and meet you by the main entrance.'

The corridors of WEDA were buzzing as everyone rushed about preparing for the showcase. Tilly made her way outside. Cassandra was waiting by the main entrance, huddled inside a fur-trimmed parka against the cold. Tilly's mum and dad were making their way up the driveway from the car park. Great, this was just what Tilly needed – an awkward family reunion in front of the ice queen.

'What are you doing here?' Tilly asked.

'What's it to you?' Cassandra snapped.

Tilly bit her tongue. There was no way she was going to have yet another falling out with Cassandra right before their showcase performance – and right in front of her mum. She walked past Cassandra to meet her parents.

'Hey, Mum. Hey, Dad.'

'Hello, love,' said her dad.

'Your hair!' her mum exclaimed.

Tilly sighed. She'd kept her hair lavender for the showcase. Everyone else seemed to love it.

'I think it looks very nice,' her dad said, giving her a hug.

'But – it's purple!' her mum exclaimed.

'Lavender, actually,' Tilly muttered, instantly wanting to kick herself. She mustn't answer her mum back today. She mustn't do anything to make her annoyed. Or more annoyed than she already looked. As the three of them started walking towards the main building Tilly avoided looking in Cassandra's direction. Maybe if she didn't see her she could pretend she wasn't there.

'So, Miss Murphy sent me your latest coursework results,' Tilly's mum said as they reached the steps and came within earshot of Cassandra. 'They really aren't good enough, Tilly, especially now you're supposed to be getting extra support. I'd been expecting to see a much bigger improvement.'

Tilly thought back to all the times Cassandra had mocked her for being stupid. She must be loving hearing her mum talk to her like this.

'Miss Murphy said it would take a while for me to get my grades up,' Tilly muttered, her face burning.

'Yes, well she would say that, wouldn't she?'

Tilly stared at her mum. 'What do you mean?'

'She doesn't want to lose our fees.'

Tilly's heart sank. So her mum didn't even believe that Miss Murphy wanted to help. She thought she was just after their money. As Tilly walked back past Cassandra she couldn't help glancing at her. But to her surprise Cassandra wasn't smirking. She actually looked slightly embarrassed, and was staring down at the floor.

'Maybe we should leave this conversation until after the show, darling,' Tilly's dad said to her mum. 'I'm sure Tilly has to go and limber up – or whatever it is you dancers do.' He looked at Tilly and grinned.

Tilly felt a loving but sad pang. If only her mum was as laidback and easy-going as her dad. Life would be so much simpler.

'OK.' Her mum sighed. 'But we will be having this conversation straight after the show.'

Tilly nodded glumly.

After she'd shown her parents to the canteen so they could get a coffee while they waited, she went to the dressing room to get changed. She and Cassandra were sharing a dressing room and their costumes – black skinny jeans and vest tops – were hanging on a rail by the door. Normally, Tilly felt excited when she put on her outfit for a show but not today. Today she felt nothing but dread. Even putting on her make-up didn't make her feel any better. Just as she'd put the finishing touches to her eyeliner Cassandra came in with a face like thunder and slammed her bag down on the dressing table.

'You OK?' Tilly muttered.

'Not really.' Cassandra sat down on the stool

in front of the mirror and stared, stony-faced at her reflection. As always, her hair and skin were flawless, but her eyes looked slightly puffy, like she'd been crying.

'What's up?'

'Let's just say you're not the only one with an evil dictator for a mother.'

'Oh.' Tilly took a moment to absorb this latest development. She vaguely remembered Billie saying something last term about having seen Cassandra's mum being mean to her. 'Sorry to hear that.'

'Yeah, well. I'm not going to let mine get to me and you'd better not let yours get to you either. I'm not having you ruin our dance.' Cassandra glared at Tilly but her eyes were glassy with tears.

'I'm not going to ruin our dance. No way!' Tilly replied. Cassandra was making her feel angry but it was good. Anger she could use – she could channel it into her dance. It was a way better energy than doubt or despair.

'Good.' Cassandra got her make-up bag out

and put it on the dressing table. 'Let's show those dictators what we're made of.'

As Tilly nodded she felt the weirdest urge to laugh. She'd never in a million years have thought that she'd find something to bond with Cassandra about. And she'd never have guessed it would be her mum.

Tilly and Cassandra's dance was the final act in the showcase. After what felt like an eternity waiting backstage, they were called to the wings. Cassandra looked really nervous and extra pale in the darkness.

'Remember what you said in the dressing room,' Tilly said, hardly able to believe she was about to give her arch enemy a pep-talk. 'We're going to show them what we can do, right?'

Cassandra nodded.

'So no trying to make me look bad or stealing the limelight. We're in this together, OK?'

'OK.' Cassandra gave her a weak smile. 'Tilly?'

'Yes?'

'I'm so –'

But before she could say any more one of the stagehands gestured to them to go on.

Tilly and Cassandra made their way on to the stage. Two spotlights burned down on them, making it impossible to see any of the faces in the crowd. Tilly thought of all the potential investors sitting in the front row.

She thought of how much good WEDA could do with their money. If this was her last day at the academy then she was going to make it count. She was going to dance like she'd never danced before and make Mrs Jones and Miss Murphy and Mr Marlo proud.

The music began and Cassandra started dancing her opening steps. Tilly focused fully as she waited for her cue. She could sense a difference in Cassandra, in the way she was dancing. For the first time ever she was properly connecting to Tilly, dancing for her and with her, not against her. As Tilly danced her response to Cassandra it felt as if they were building something together instead of creating their own separate dances. Their routines wove together seamlessly and it felt so good. Tilly's feet tapped faster, stronger and freer than ever before. Instead of feeling gangly and awkward, her long legs felt powerful and able to cover so much space. Faster and faster and faster they both tapped. Tilly could feel the excitement and laughter from the audience rising like a cloud in the auditorium. She drank in the energy and let it fuel her feet, allowing her to be more and more animated with her slapstick moments. And then, finally, the dance reached its climax. Tilly and Cassandra picked up and blew on their right feet like they were smoking pistols. There was a moment's stunned silence, then the crowd burst into laughter and applause.

'Oh my God, they're giving us a standing ovation!' Tilly gasped as she stared out into the audience. She turned to look at Cassandra and Cassandra smiled. And for once it wasn't an arrogant smirk or a knowing grin – it was a proper, genuinely happy smile.

'We showed them,' she said in Tilly's ear. 'We really showed them.'

But as soon as they got back to the dressing room, Tilly's euphoria drained away. Now she had to meet her parents in the canteen for the dreaded conversation. She quickly changed into sweatpants and a hoodie and made her way down there.

Her parents were waiting for her by the door to the canteen. Her dad was beaming, her mum's face was expressionless. All around them the other students and their parents milled about, buzzing with excitement from the show.

'You were incredible,' Tilly's dad said, pulling her in for a hug. 'Well done! I'm so proud of you.'

'Thanks, Dad.' Tilly looked at her mum hopefully.

'Yes, you were very good,' her mum said, slightly stiffly.

'Come on, let's get some food,' Tilly said numbly, even though she'd completely lost her appetite.

As they made their way over to the buffet counter Tilly saw Billie and her mum and her uncle laughing and joking at a table. She thought about having to leave Billie and her heart almost split in two. This was so unfair. Why couldn't her mum see that this was where she belonged?

When they'd got their food Tilly led her parents over to a table in the far corner. She didn't want anyone overhearing what was about to come.

'That really was a very good performance,' Tilly's mum said, pouring her bottle of juice into a glass.

Tilly felt a pinprick of hope.

'Your dancing has improved enormously.'

'Thank you.' Tilly could hardly breathe. Was her mum about to back down?

'But I'm just worried that it's come at the expense of your academic subjects. Are you putting so much time into your dance that you don't have any left over for things like Maths and English? And now we've established that your dyslexia is worse than you were letting on we need to make sure you have the extra time you need.'

'It's not like that, Mum, it's –' But before Tilly

could say any more she spotted Andre heading towards their table. He was wearing a gold tracksuit and a bright green baseball cap. He looked super-excited. Tilly panicked. Her parents hadn't met Andre yet. She wasn't exactly sure what her mum would make of him.

'OMG, Tillz. We have a major GV situation!' Andre exclaimed as he got to their table and slammed his laptop down in front of Tilly. Then he looked at her parents. 'Sorry, I'm Andre. I'm sure you've heard all about me.' Andre opened his laptop as Tilly's mum and dad looked at each other blankly.

'What's a GV situation?' Tilly muttered.

'Going viral.' Andre turned the laptop so that it was facing Tilly's mum. 'Take a look at this, Mamma Tillz. Your daughter is amazing.'

Tilly shifted closer to her mum so she could see the screen. It was on Tyler Joseph's Twitter page and a video titled *How to Slay an Audition*. Andre pressed play and an image of Tilly appeared. It was from her audition. Tilly watched, speechless, as Andre turned up the volume and her spoken-word poem began playing through the speakers. It was the first time Tilly had seen what the audition looked like from the audience's point of view. There was no denying that the combination of spoken word, images and dance was incredibly powerful but Tilly couldn't help seeing it through her mum's eyes. What would she be making of it all?

'What is this?' her mum asked. 'Is that your voice?'

'Yes,' Tilly replied. 'It's from an audition I did recently.'

'Whose words are you reading?' her mum said.

'Mine,' Tilly answered. Confused thoughts filled her mind. Why had Tyler shared the video of her audition on Twitter? What did this mean?

'My freedom's creative bubble popped, by judgements opposing my way of being.' Tilly's voice rang out from the laptop.

Tilly couldn't bring herself to look at her mum. She kept staring blankly at the screen.

'This false system tortures a dyslexic mind to strive for its impossible perfection. So, while I wait for you to notice? I'm taking my time to shine. Cos my time to shine? Is now.'

Tilly held her breath. She sounded so angry in the poem. So hurt and raw. She glanced at her mum.

'I – I need to get some fresh air,' her mum said, standing up.

'Mum, are you OK?' Tilly stood up too.

But her mum didn't answer, she just hurried towards the door.

Tilly raced after her. 'Mum! Wait.'

Her mum stood just outside the canteen, her hand clamped to her mouth.

'What is it? What's wrong?' Tilly said.

'Did you mean it?' her mum said. 'The things you said in the poem. Is that how you feel? Is that how I make you feel?'

Tilly nodded. 'My dyslexia feels like a prison, Mum,' she said quietly. 'But my friends and my teachers – they're helping me find my way out. They got me to do spoken-word poetry instead of written and I really love it. I'm not stupid, Mum, and I'm not lazy. I've been working so hard, honestly.' Tilly felt a lump growing in her throat. She looked down at the ground.

'Did you do the artwork in that video too?'

Tilly nodded.

'Oh, Tilly.' Her mum took hold of her hand. 'I'm so sorry. I just – it's so hard for me. I come from such an academic background. Education is so important to me. Your father says I'm a boring old fuddy-duddy but I can't help it. It's how my parents were and their parents before them. We've always been such an academic family and then you came along and . . .'

Tilly felt tears welling in her eyes. 'Do you wish you'd never had me?'

'No!' her mum exclaimed, taking hold of her arm. 'Of course not. My goodness, when I was watching you on that stage today I was so proud. I couldn't take my eyes off you. I couldn't believe that a lawyer like me could be mum to such a – such a creative tour de force.'

Tilly wasn't exactly sure what a tour de force was but it sounded as if her mum meant it as a compliment, so that was definitely good.

'Hello!'

Tilly and her mum jumped at the sound of Miss Murphy's voice and turned to see her striding towards them.

'Just the people I was looking for,' Miss Murphy said with a warm smile. 'Wonderful performance in the showcase, Tilly.' Miss Murphy turned to her mum. 'You must be so proud.'

Tilly's mum nodded. 'I am.'

'Now, about that meeting you wanted,' Miss Murphy continued. 'Do you fancy popping up to my office for a chat?'

Tilly's mum shook her head and Tilly's stomach lurched.

'That won't be necessary,' her mum said. 'I've seen enough today to know that this is definitely the right place for my daughter.'

'What? But . . .' Tilly spluttered.

Her mum smiled. 'Obviously I'd like to be kept up to date with how she's getting on in her lessons but I'm more than happy for her to continue at WEDA.'

Tilly threw her arms around her. 'Mum! That's sick!'

Her mum looked confused. 'What's sick?'

'I mean good. Sick means good.'

'Sick means good?' Tilly's mum echoed, looking even more confused.

Miss Murphy laughed. 'Young people today speak in a whole different language. You should hear some of the things my son says. Ah, speak of the devil.'

Andre peered around the door to the canteen looking really anxious. 'Is everything OK?'

Tilly nodded.

'Come on.' Miss Murphy took hold of Tilly's mum's arm. 'Let's go and get a cup of coffee and leave these youngsters to their "sick talk".'

'Sick talk?' Andre looked after Miss Murphy, horrified. 'OMG, she's so embarrassing!' He turned back to Tilly, his eyes wide. 'Did it work?'

'Did what work?'

'Did the video convince your mum to let you stay here?'

Tilly stared at him. 'Is that why you showed it to her?'

'Of course! She'd be mad to not recognize just how talented you are.'

Tilly grinned. 'Yes, it did.'

'Thank God! When she ran out of the canteen I swear I thought I was going to throw up with nerves.' Andre took a deep breath. 'What happened? Did she burst into tears and beg your forgiveness like in the movies?'

'Er, no. But she did say I can stay here.'

'Oh my God, that's so awesome.' Andre threw his arms round her. 'Wow, this really has been your lucky day. You slayed your performance with the ice queen, you got your mum to let you stay at WEDA *and* you landed a role in a video for one of the dopest bands ever.'

'Wait, what? I got the job?'

'Of course you got the job, doofus. Why do you think Tyler Joseph tweeted your audition video?'

'I don't know. I didn't have time to find out, did I? I was too busy trying to stop my mum from having a nervous breakdown.'

Andre gave a sigh. 'Girlfriend, you so need to check your emails.'

Tilly took her phone from her pocket, her fingers trembling. There, in her inbox, was an email from the music video people – with the title *CONGARTULATOINS*.

'Oh, Andre!' Tilly gasped as she read the email and deciphered just enough words to work out it was good news. 'I did it! I got the job!'

'What's going on?' Billie said, rushing out of the canteen, looking really worried. 'Tilly, are you OK? I saw you running out after your mum. And she's just gone back inside with Miss Murphy. Is everything all right?'

Tilly nodded. 'Yes, it's all good. Everything's good.'

'It's never been gooder,' Andre said. 'Is gooder even a word? Oh well, it is now.'

'My mum says I can stay at WEDA!' Tilly told Billie.

'And she got the video job for Twenty One Pilots,' Andre added. 'Tilly, that is – not her mum – that would be so weird.'

'Oh wow, that's amazing!' Billie exclaimed, hugging Tilly. 'Come on, you've got to tell Raf and MJ – they're so worried you're about to be taken out of WEDA.'

They hurried back into the canteen and over to a table by the juice bar where Raf and MJ were sitting.

As soon as Tilly told them her news they leaped to their feet and all of Il Bello grabbed Tilly in a group hug.

'I couldn't have done it without you guys,' Tilly said, feeling so happy she thought her heart might burst.

'Yep, true dat,' Andre said. 'Big up, Il Bello. The best street crew in the entire universe!'

As they all started laughing Mrs Jones walked into the canteen and rapped her cane on the floor. The whole place fell silent.

'Students and parents, I have some very good news,' Mrs Jones said. 'I've just come from a meeting with the investors who watched the showcase and I'm delighted to inform you that they were so impressed they've pledged almost double of what we were asking.'

A cheer rang out around the canteen.

'Thank you so much for all of your hard work and dedication,' Mrs Jones continued. 'Because of you, we'll not only be able to install the solar panels to the studios but we'll also be able to offer more bursaries than ever in the next school year. I think you all deserve a massive round of applause.'

As cheering rang out around the canteen Tilly searched the crowd for her mum. She spotted her sitting with her dad and Miss Murphy clapping and smiling like she really, truly meant it. As Tilly tried to process all the events of the day – her tap routine with Cassandra, her mum letting her stay at WEDA, and landing the music video job – she felt excitement burning inside of her as bright and powerful as the sun. And then she realized something that made her tingle from head to toe. The words from her poem had actually come true. Her time to shine was now.

TILLY'S SPOKEN-WORD POEM

Like a vacant scroll through the timelines of social
    media,
waiting for a like.
Finding safety in an emoji,
wishing that life were as simple
as the smile I portray to an online world
that's never truly paying attention.
When will it be my time to shine?
The spray of my paint releases me from this prison
    that I'm in.
This impossibility to fit in.
So harshly judged.
My positivity never stands out positively.
My freedom's creative bubble popped
by judgements opposing my way of being.
The true me goes unnoticed,
dwarfed by letters,
blocking me from my unique intelligence.
When will it be my time to shine?

When fear takes my tongue I quiver,

shrinking back into my box of difference.

Be you, be fearless, be authentic, be weird, be real.

Be the flight of the bumblebee

spreading a beautiful crew's message to the masses.

A purpose-driven life inspires me

to embrace what others deem unacceptable.

All could be gone in a moment of unavoidable

   guidance,

willing me to be a clone of praise.

When will it ever be my time to shine?

Stay strong, tiny dancer, and be the crazy diamond

   you know you are.

A rare gem of honest perspective from a life.

This false system tortures a dyslexic mind

to strive for its impossible perfection.

So, while I wait for you to notice?

I'm taking my time to shine.

Cos my time to shine?

Is now.

KIMBERLY WYATT rose to fame as a member of one of the biggest girl groups of all time, the Pussycat Dolls. Together they sold over 55 million records worldwide, before coming to an end in 2010. Now a firm favourite on our UK screens, Kimberly has appeared on scores of high-profile TV shows like SKY 1's *Got to Dance*, as well as CBBC's *Taking the Next Step*. She was crowned winner of BBC1's *Celebrity Masterchef* in 2015.

Passionate about keeping fit, eating well and being the 'best version of yourself', Kimberly has fast become a positive role model and fitness inspiration for many. She tours schools with her 'Well Fit' campaign with the Youth Sport Trust, promoting the physical and mental wellbeing messages that tie in to her books. In 2014 Kimberly became a mother to daughter, Willow.

Q&A with Kimberly

What made you want to write the WEDA series?

WEDA is my way of giving back to the next generation of dreamers and doers like me. I love dance. I love that dance brings people of all different cultures together. I love the determination dance inspires through its disciplines and I love the confidence and sense of achievement you get from doing dance moves and choreography. The WEDA series is based on my own experiences training, competing and auditioning, and the many dancers and teachers that have inspired me along the way.

Do you share experiences with Billie?

Billie's experiences at WEDA are based on my life as a dancer, coming from very little money, working extra hard to make my dreams come true. We share the battle to fit in and the challenge to stand out, the struggle with self-doubt and the fight to unlock our inner street beast. The dance world is tough and the anxieties and stresses that go along with it are reflections of my own dance journey.

Who was your favourite character to come up with?

Andre was great fun! Andre is based on a lot of dancers
I danced with or worked with while living in Los Angeles.
Cheeky, fun and full of energy, his confidence is infectious
and his ability to embrace his eccentricities is inspiring.
I love him.

*What advice would you give to someone who wants
to become a performer?*

Be you, Be fearless, Be authentic! Nobody can do *you*
like you can!

Did you have any favourite books when growing up?

I loved the Nancy Drew series, *Charlotte's Web* was the
first book that made me cry. *James and the Giant Peach*
was the ultimate fantasy and *The Good Earth* by Pearl S.
Buck was a life-changing read as a teen.

Be you, be fearless, be authentic!

The new series from international superstar, wellbeing guru and Pussycat Doll, **Kimberly Wyatt**

Join Billie and her friends on a fierce and empowering journey to dance stardom.

EGMONT